www.ChloeEmile.com

Violette Nights in Paris

A French Kiss Romantic Comedy

CHLOE EMILE

This is a work of fiction. Names, characters, organizations, places, events, and incidents are either products of the author's imagination or are used fictitiously. Some locations in Paris are real, and others are fictitious.

ISBN-13: 978-1987859157
ISBN-10: 1987859154

CONTENTS

CHAPTER ONE

*I*n a city somewhere in Europe, Mathieu sprawls out on the couch in the VIP lounge backstage of the concert hall. His band, Les Slinks, has just performed the final show of their scheduled European Union tour. All the cities and towns blur together after being on the road so often, and some days Mathieu can't even remember his own name.

"That was our best show yet. I can't believe we're headed home, for a few weeks at least." Guillaume, their drummer, shouts in celebration as he grabs a beer from the bar and takes a long swig from the bottle.

Mathieu, the ultrasexy, brown-haired, blue-eyed lead singer lets out an exasperated sigh.

"Dude, what are you mopey about?" the bass guitarist, Olivier, asks him from across the upscale lounge.

The entire band and, well, anyone who knows Mathieu is used to his major mood swings. If he wasn't the brooding artist type, one would think that he was borderline bipolar. Scratch that—they would think he was full-on bipolar.

"Nothing, man," Mathieu retorts, although he doesn't want to admit that he is exhausted to his core, and not just from being on tour.

"We just finished a record-selling tour, our songs are skyrocketing on the charts, and everyone thinks that you're a god or something." Olivier snaps his guitar shut in its black leather case.

Mathieu thinks he detects a hint of jealousy in Olivier's voice. The lead singer is the face of the band, and Olivier loves attention. That's just the way it is with Les Slinks and every other band out there.

Olivier sets the guitar case down on the ground, walks over to the couch, and crouches down next to Mathieu.

"Besides, look at all these gorgeous girls here. I bet you can take any of them home tonight. Hell, if you're lucky enough, I bet you can take two home with you," Olivier says with a conniving laugh.

Mathieu rolls his eyes at his buddy because Olivier is the textbook definition of sleazy. This hypothesis is only confirmed for the millionth time when Olivier stakes his claim on both the redhead in a skimpy black dress with more cleavage showing than a Victoria's Secret catalog and the girl with the long, curly blond hair.

Mathieu has seen this side of Olivier more times than he could count on his hands and toes multiplied by a dozen. He and Olivier grew up together, became fast friends in the second grade, and have remained a close duo ever since.

Mathieu finds it fascinating to watch Olivier try to woo whichever girl he fancies for the evening, because Olivier was about as nerdy as a guy could get growing up, aside from Mathieu, that is. In fact, Mathieu was probably the dorkiest dweeb in all of Montmartre with his giant tortoiseshell glasses and moody outbursts. It is nothing short of a miracle that they went from there to here.

His mom, a free-spirited, flower-child, painter type, was determined to make sure their family represented high values, even if she eschewed the bourgeoisie lifestyle.

Mathieu inherited her wild side, while some of his brothers, such as Alain and Luc, took after their father's more reserved personality. Mathieu grew up in a home full of love and laughter, and his parents were the epitome of opposites falling in love. Just like complementary colors such as yellow and violet, Mathieu's parents enhanced the qualities of one another.

In high school and university, Mathieu transformed himself, creating a look and an attitude to go with it. As for his style, he can usually be found in his signature uniform, a rock star's uniform. His closet and suitcases are full of graphic T-shirts, leather jackets, distressed jeans, sneakers, and cool shades. These days, the cool clothes are just for the stage. When he's just being plain Mathieu, he sticks to the distressed jeans and T-shirts.

Now that he is a rock star, Mathieu is astonished on a daily basis for how much excess and waste exists in this world around him and how much greed and envy is present on any given day.

One time, in the heat of a moment on stage, he ripped his shirt off and threw it into the crowd. Naturally the crowd went insane, and he could only imagine what the decibel level registered at with all the fans chanting his name: *Mathieu! Mathieu! Mathieu!* The lights were blaring in their faces, the crowd was hard to see in the dark arena, but he felt alive. His music was his passion, and the reaction it garnered excited him. He was also the cause of their reaction, and their adoration was thunderous.

The next day, to his utter disgust, he found out that the shirt he took off on stage was up for bid on eBay. People were literally betting thousands on his torn shirt.

The entire band was weirded out about this incident, but they all felt as though they had truly made it in the music business after that. People either worshiped them, wanted to be them, or be as close to them as possible, even if it meant owning a sweaty, gross T-shirt.

Mathieu gathers his thoughts and sits up on the couch to look his friend right in the eye. It's as though he's gone from morose to passionate with the flip of a light switch.

"But, Ollie, don't you want something more? Something meaningful?"

Olivier whips out his cell phone and pulls up the app were he keeps his notes.

"I feel a song coming on," Olivier says with a singsong tone of excitement in his voice.

"Well, I don't," Mathieu responds with irritation. "These girls are beautiful, but there has to be so much more to this than taking home one girl on Thursday and a different one on Saturday."

"Oh, don't get all serious on me. I'm just having fun."

Tonight, Mathieu senses that Olivier doesn't feel like playing therapist to him. He just wants a good time, although Mathieu sees a good existential conversation as fun.

"Do what you want, bud," Olivier says and walks back to the girls.

Mathieu lies back down on the couch and watches his friend with pure amazement. As the redhead laughs at Olivier's corny jokes, Mathieu finally allows himself to come to a realization that he has been holding in for a long, long time.

The success he and Les Slinks have created, which is no doubt more than most bands dream of, has been phenomenal. With one record in French and one in English, international fame, tours in Europe, and opening for major name headliners in the States, Mathieu should be radiating pride and arrogance.

But he is not.

To Mathieu, his music is art, with or without the crowds. He feels the same way about arena crowds as he did banging pots, pans, and anything else with his siblings when he was younger.

He hasn't even been drinking that much, but all of the sudden, he feels as if he is being suffocated, as if a boa contractor has wrapped its slinky body around his neck without any intention of releasing its prey. It feels like a panic attack, something that is becoming more frequent. His heart races, fear engulfs his mind, and he cannot do anything besides just breathe through it. He knows the feeling will pass, but during this particular instance, he is fed up with feeling this way.

There has to be more, he tells himself. Olivier, Marcel, and Guillaume certainly don't seem to feel this soul-crushing anxiety.

What Mathieu needs are wide-open spaces and fresh air. Every cell of his body is craving it now. He knows he needs to get out of this lounge, out of whatever city this is, and somewhere where there are fewer people, fewer commotions, and fewer demands. At least for a little while.

He finally thinks that perhaps he understands where all of this tug-and-pull war of emotions is coming from, not that he could ever admit this to anyone. In this world of excess and waste and money, he takes after his mother more than he thinks. Is it possible that perhaps Mathieu feels like his biggest success is his biggest failure?

Mathieu dashes over to the bar area. "Excuse me, do you have a piece of paper and pen I can borrow? Anything will work."

The bartender pulls a piece of receipt paper from the cash register and hands it along with a pen over to Mathieu, who is growing more impatient by the second.

It's well past midnight, although Mathieu is unsure of the exact time. He grabs the paper and pen and walks to the far side of the counter where he has a little bit of space.

He sits on one of the red leather stools, and in quick handwriting, Mathieu scribbles, *I have to go. Personal matters. I'll meet you in Paris in two months or so.*

Mathieu signs it as if he were giving an autograph for an enthusiastic fan—just Mathieu, no last name.

He scans the room, skipping over Olivier and his two girls, and pauses when he sees Les Slinks' drummer, Guillaume, chugging down his beer.

Feeling a rush of adrenaline for the first time in what feels like a lifetime, Mathieu heads straight for Guillaume, who appears to be on at least his fifth or sixth drink for the night, and presses the note into his hand before quickly walking off.

Out of the corner of his eye, Mathieu sees Guillaume read the note, but Guillaume is so drunk that it takes him more seconds than it should to process what the note entails.

As Mathieu exits the door, he catches the last scene as it starts to unfold in the stifling lounge. He sees Guillaume showing the others the note.

He doesn't wait to see any more. They are probably scratching their heads and trying to figure out if the note says what they think it says. Mathieu's handwriting is appalling. They probably think it is one of his practical jokes. He almost wants to laugh at the thought.

He can only imagine the chaos of the situation. Les Slinks can't be Les Slinks without their Mathieu. He is Les Slinks. He knows without a doubt that their manager and record label will panic. Olivier's main concern will probably be frustration when his plans with Goldilocks and the redhead are interrupted.

And just like the speed of a lightning bolt or the Euro rail rushing into its next location, Mathieu disappears into an unknown city, at an unknown hour, with an unknown plan.

CHAPTER TWO

$\mathcal{V}$iolette Deschamps is reminded of how much she hates her hourglass figure every time she looks at herself in a full-length mirror. She hates her hips, and her hair has a single curl that she straightens with a flatiron on a daily basis. She has been doing it for so long that the habit is officially as second nature as breathing. She puts on her fake pearl earrings, a signature look for her, and lets out an exasperated sigh as she takes a final look at herself before heading out the door for work.

While there is no way to hide her curves, she certainly takes giant strides in not drawing attention to herself. Wearing simple, boring frocks, cardigans, and sensible shoes is her clothing motto. She often dresses like someone heading to an old-fashioned tea party and not the late-twenties girl that she is. It's not that she isn't fashionable; it's just that she doesn't feel comfortable having a lot of attention on her, especially on her body.

After a quick glance to make sure she is presentable, Violette flips open her work calendar to see what the day holds. On the docket she sees a meeting with the Gardiniers, a young couple looking for their first row home on a shoestring budget in the suburbs. While it can be tricky, Violette loves the game of chasing good deals for homes. In her profession as a realtor for Domaines D'Elegance in the heart of Paris, Violette aims to make sure her clients buy houses that give them the wow factor while staying within their budgets. Violette is one of the lucky ones who genuinely gains satisfaction from her work.

However, her true dream job is interior design. She went to university to become an interior designer and, due to circumstances out of her control, had to return home and quit her studies.

Fortunately, Violette is good at real estate sales, and each month, she brings in a comfortable salary. She easily covers both her expenses and the expenses of her mother, which lately have been skyrocketing due to her mother's poor health with Alzheimer's disease.

Despite the caretaking responsibilities without much needed respite, Violette continues to look for beauty in the mundane. Just recently, she was able to buy an apartment just south of Paris. The place needed some updating, that's for sure, but Violette felt magic when she walked through the doors for the first time. It didn't hurt that it was in her dream neighborhood. The modest apartment is certainly not a mansion by any means, but it's open, airy, and well decorated. Violette spent hours poring over online pictures and magazines and then spent even more hours bargain hunting, antiquing, and completing do-it-yourself projects to create her own personal oasis. It's a secret hobby of hers.

One of her secret desires is to have a reality show where she gets to renovate houses, make exquisite benches out of simple pallet boards, and turn antiques into modern works of art. She may not like to dress herself, but she loves for her environment to be a place of beauty. Her philosophy is that the world around you is a springboard for inspiration.

Ready for the day, Violette heads over to La Rue de Baie where Clara and Jared Gardinier are hoping to become homeowners.

Violette arrives a few minutes early and luckily finds one last spot on the street to park.

Unfortunately, she has to parallel park, one of her least favorite things to do ever. She has this little quirk where she will say three Hail Mary prayers and hope to God she doesn't slam into either the car behind her or in front of her. She is convinced it will happen one of these days.

Fortunately, she glides right into the narrow spot, unbuckles her seatbelt, turns the key to stop the engine, and hops out.

As she walks up to unlock the home for the Gardiniers, she sees that the couple has beaten her there. She finds this a little unfortunate because she always likes the opportunity to go in before the clients, turn all the lights on, and make sure there is nothing weird lurking in one of the rooms, like a bag of trash, an unflushed toilet, or a dead person.

Okay, okay, not really a dead person, but Violette does have a wild imagination. Any of those things might potentially turn off a buyer, so a real estate agent cannot ever be too prepared.

"Violette, hi!" Clara says eagerly, while Jared gives a friendly wave.

"*Bonjour,*" Violette calls out with a professional and friendly tone.

"We have the best news ever," Clara beams.

Violette has a feeling she knows what is coming next, with a sinking feeling in her stomach.

"You tell her, Jared," Clara semi-whispers while grabbing her husband's hand.

Before he can get the words out, Clara practically shouts out the news that they are expecting their first baby.

Violette is pretty sure this will be the first of many little munchkins. She owns up to the fact that there is a teeny, tiny chance she is experiencing some pangs of envy.

Single with the responsibility of taking care of an ailing parent and no other family, Violette often wishes there were someone out there for her, but so far, the tarot cards all show a single cat lady, which is a problem because she doesn't even like cats. Maybe she'll get a dog instead.

Those thoughts are quickly brushed aside as Violette acts professional and feigns joy for the couple. In a way, it is exciting and Violette genuinely wants to share their happiness.

But she's human and a little jealous—the understatement of the century. How fair is it that these two gorgeous people have this perfect life? She is not a gambling lady, but if she were, she would put up a high-stakes bet that both their parents are still alive and healthy.

Sick mom, father passed, as many dating prospects as a brick wall, and ticking ovaries. Sometimes, life doesn't feel fair.

But Violette can't let herself succumb to jealousy. "Jared, Clara, I'm thrilled for you guys!"

She embraces each of them with a double-cheek kiss and steps up her real estate game.

"Does this mean a bigger house is in order? More beds? More baths? A larger yard?" Violette asks with a half-serious, half-joking tone.

She regrets saying this. Their focus is supposed to be on this house, which is a pretty good buy. She quickly recovers by saying that this house might still be perfect for their needs.

Jared, who is clearly the quieter of the two, quickly speaks up, "Under no circumstances will we go above budget."

She is ninety-nine percent sure that the comment is directed right at his wife.

"I know budget is a concern," Violette says. "The location is ideal and the schools around here are excellent." She holds onto the doorknob and before she turns it, offers a warning to the Gardiniers. "Just be aware of one thing. This house is under budget, but it does need some work."

"Under budget sounds great," Jared says.

Clara, on the other hand, does not look quite impressed. In fact, Violette swears she can see her lip starting to pout just a little bit. Violette stifles the urge both to roll her eyes and laugh.

While she might have a sunny disposition, Violette has a little self-talk with herself and warns her brain to be nice, especially since she is more than aware that princess Clara may not like the house at first glance.

And she's right.

"This living room is horrid," Clara says with an appalled look.

"Freeze, right there," Violette says. "I agree, right now, this living room is quite horrid. You've got me there, Clara. But look at these wood beams in the ceiling. The exposed brick surrounding the fireplace."

She pauses and lets them soak it in before continuing. "New paint, refinished hardwood floors, patching this giant hole in the wall."

Violette once again takes a silent breath and then suggests maybe even tearing down the wall between the dining room and living room to create more of an open-concept living plan.

With a definitive voice, Clara wastes no time in saying that she cannot picture it.

Jared, on the other hand, might, just might, be swinging for Team Fixer-Upper and says that it could potentially work, depending on the price of the contractors.

Violette leads them to the backyard, which features a large deck, fenced-in grass area—perfect for a play set!—and emphasizes that it would be marvelous for entertaining.

For some reason, clients are always so concerned with having space to entertain, although when it comes down to it, how much entertaining do house hunters really do?

Violette thinks they are hooked with their backyard space, which really is stunning, and then takes them to the upstairs where all the bedrooms are.

"Well, at least all the bedrooms are on the same floor," Clara adds, which was one of the top items on her wish list.

"This level looks like it will need some remodeling as well," Jared states.

Violette can see him trying to tally up the numbers in his head. "Yep, some remodeling does need to happen to update and modernize this. The good news about any renovation project is that you get to personalize every detail from the tile, to the wall color, to the whatever you would like."

After she shows them the house, she gives them a few minutes of privacy to walk back through the home and talk among themselves. Violette lets them know that she will be waiting outside and they can come find her when she's ready.

About five minutes later, the couple comes out and Violette asks the question she asks every couple once they see a house. "So, now that you have seen the house, how much do you think it costs?"

"Maybe three hundred thousand euros?" Clara guesses.

"I would say closer to two hundred eighty thousand euros," Jared says.

With a smile of satisfaction, Violette reveal that price is actually two hundred twenty-five thousand euros, giving them enough for renovation costs in their dream neighborhood.

"This certainly gives us a few things to think about," Jared says.

The three say their good-byes, the dream couple drives off, and Violette is off to spend the evening with someone who doesn't even know her name.

CHAPTER THREE

$\mathcal{V}$iolette types up the last e-mail for the day, one to the Gardiniers answering a question about an interior design recommendation. She hits send, grabs her purse, and hits the road to go visit her mother at the hospice center.

On the way out the door, her boss and friend, Jean-Phillipe, asks if she has a minute to stop at the patisserie two storefronts down from Domaines D'Elegance to talk business.

Jean-Phillipe, an older family man in his fifties, has taken Violette under his wing both professionally and personally. He gave her a job as a secretary when she quit university to take care of her mother. Sure, when she took it, she knew it was a pity offering, but she was desperate. And determined.

She helped out the agents, learned the trade, got her realtor certification, and she owes most of her success to Old Man Jean-Phillipe.

"Sure," Violette says. "That would be great. I am a bit hungry."

"Let's go," Jean-Phillipe responds, and they start walking down the street. "So, Violette, I just wanted to check in."

"Is everything okay? Are my sales not above the projected goals for the year?"

"No, no, my dear. Violette, you know you are one of the best employees. I just wanted to see how everything else was going for you. I try not to pry, but I can't help but worry about you like you were one of my own," Jean-Phillipe says with genuine interest.

Jean-Phillipe holds the door for Violette as she steps under the red-and-white-striped awning and is instantly warmed by the aroma of pastries and baked goods. She lets herself inhale the sweet smells of the cookies, croissants, cakes, and petit fours.

No one is in line ahead of them, so Violette asks the young girl with the ponytail and striped apron working the counter, "Do you have any almond croissants, *mademoiselle*?"

The young woman says they just took a fresh batch out of the oven and goes to the back to grab one.

"They have always been your favorite, haven't they?" Jean-Phillipe asks.

"You know it," Violette responds with a smile.

Jean-Phillipe orders a butter croissant, and they grab one of the tiny tables sitting by the window.

Violette sinks her teeth into her warm croissant and instantly feels better.

"So I have a proposition for you, Vi," he starts, sounding nervous.

Jean-Phillipe is the only one who calls her Vi.

"I don't like the sound of this already," Violette says cautiously, picking an almond off the top of her croissant.

Propositions usually end up in more work and less money.

"Just hear me out," Jean-Phillipe says.

Violette would never say this out loud, but she is thinking, *Holy crap, please don't let this get awkward or sexual or weird or...*

Before her mind can wander any further, Jean-Phillipe continues on. "My nephew is

27

coming into town, and I thought you might like to meet him. You know, show him around, that kind of thing. He is in town for a job interview, a very good opportunity, I might add, and I think you would get along fine. Better than fine, actually."

"Are you trying to set me up?" Violette asks as she squints her eyes, already knowing the answer.

"I would never!" Jean-Phillipe says with a boyish grin.

"Jean-Phillipe," she says in her best warning voice with a hint of humor. "I'll think about it, but right now, I need to head to visit Mom and get her ready for bed. Thanks for the croissant."

"Just think about it, Vi, please? Even just coffee or tea, I'll throw in one of these almond croissants to sweeten the deal!" Jean-Phillipe says, knowing they are her weakness.

"Good-bye, Jean-Phillipe." Violette rolls her eyes jokingly, grabs her bag, and heads back out the door and into the evening light.

In her little car, she pulls into the front of the hospice center where her mom is staying for Alzheimer's care. Despite the illness and death and sorrow lurking behind the walls, this center is surprisingly cheery. Fresh flowers and white rocking chairs line the front entry way and in a weird, sick, twisted way, this place has become her second home.

She hits the buzzer and waits for a nurse to let her into the building.

Luckily, Nadine, her favorite evening nurse, greets her. They exchange kisses on the each side of the cheek.

"Hello, Violette," Nadine says warmly.

"How is she doing today, Nadine?" Violette asks, hoping for good news.

"Oh, honey," Nadine says with sad eyes, "I think she is about the same today. Not better, not worse."

Nadine takes Violette's hand and gives it a little squeeze. Violette is so appreciative to have her support here. Nadine's a true saint in the way that only a nurse with a heart the size of a Swiss castle can be—avoids the pity, provides the support, and doesn't sugarcoat the news.

Violette hates it when doctors and nurses sugarcoat what's going on. She would rather get the facts straight.

Violette and Nadine chat while they walk back to Lydia Deschamps's room.

"All right, Violette, holler if you need anything," Nadine says as she turns to walk back down the hallway while Violette steps inside her mom's bedroom.

"*Bonjour, maman,* it's me, Violette."

Lydia smiles, but does not say anything back to Violette. Violette knows that her mother has no idea who she is, but the smile says she welcomes the company. It's the very reason that Violette comes night after night.

Sticking to her routine, Violette grabs the hairbrush from the small nightstand drawer and begins brushing her mom's hair and wrapping the thin white strands in curlers. Her mom used to love going to the salon, and Violette makes sure her hair is done once a week. It doesn't take long, but Violette tells her about her day as she does it. She tells her about the latest apartment project, Clara and Jared Gardiniers, and Jean-Phillipe's crazy request to set her up with his nephew.

"All right, *maman,* your hair looks beautiful, just like always," she says, "and now we are going to keep reading."

A single, unexpected tear falls onto her cheek, and she wipes it away. She pulls out the old library book, settles into the recliner chair by her mother's bed, and opens the book up to the very spot they left off with yesterday.

She finishes reading the chapter aloud. Her mom is responsive in that her eyes are open and she smiles, but Violette doesn't dare ask her if she knows who she is. That affirmation would break her already cracked heart.

Finally, Violette turns on the radio to her mother's favorite oldies station and sings and hums along to a couple of songs being played before kissing her forehead and saying "I love you" to her sweet *maman*.

***

Violette walks down the long hallway of the hospice, back toward the front door, and she lets herself take in a deep breath, the kind of deep breath that women in labor or people having panic attacks take—long, slow, through the belly, and the diaphragm. While she knows her mother is going to continue her slow descent, which Violette finds unbearable, she finds comfort knowing that her mom is receiving comfortable care. She is not in pain. She is not sad. She just is.

Violette gets to the front door and sees Nadine nearby.

"You outta here?" Nadine calls out to Violette.

"Until tomorrow, at least," Violette responds.

"Girl, you need to do something fun. Loosen up! Your mom would want you to. I tell you what, if you promise to do something for you tomorrow, I'll take care of your mama's bedtime routine. I'll sing to her, read to her, all of it."

"Maybe sometime, but not tomorrow," Violette says.

Nadine shakes her head in disappointment. "Well, just think about it."

"Will do. Goodnight, Nadine," Violette says.

"Night, Violette!" Nadine hits the button to unlock the door for Violette before getting back to work organizing the medicine cart. Violette pushes the door open and heads out into the night once again.

She gets back into her little car just as it starts to drizzle and begins her short drive to her home, knowing exactly how she will spend the next few hours.

By the time she pulls into the parking garage of her building, the small drizzle has turned into a torrential downpour. While some people hate the rain, Violette thinks of rain as sensual. She sees something so relaxing in the pitter-patter of the raindrops against windows. Even now, as a grown woman, she pictures the raindrops as ballerinas, dancing on the black pavement in a one-two-three-four rhythm.

As much solace as she takes in tonight's weather, Violette is even happier to unlock the door to her house, her sanctuary, and the first thing she does is take her bra off. There is something oddly freeing about unhooking that darned undergarment. She thinks the bra is a curse against womankind, but stepping into warm pajamas is the perfect remedy for a long day full of the usual priorities and responsibilities. As someone nearing thirty, Violette's life is full of both priorities and responsibilities.

So she does what any respectable single girl would do. She pulls out a bottle of her favorite red wine, grabs her chunky knit throw blanket, and settles in on the couch, which, like everything else, she fixed. She actually found it on the side of the road but saw it had charming bones. She had a couple friends carry it up to her apartment, and they thought she was crazy until they saw the finished product. She stripped away all the old fabric, removed the nasty, dingy stuffing, and rebuilt the piece with a soft, tan fabric.

She plops down on the sofa with her latest mystery novel, her favorite genre. This is one book she can't put down, about a girl who finds hidden treasure in an underground tunnel. Plus, there is a love story in there, and Violette is a sucker for a good romance. She lives vicariously through the strong, adventurous heroines of whatever book she is engrossed in at the time.

Before she flips open the book to page 127, where she left off last night, Violette has a pang of longing. The pang is short, shorter than a blink of the eye.

For once, she wishes that she could have a little more adventure and less of a life of complacency, which is how she sees her current existence: dull, boring, and in need of a complete and total makeover.

CHAPTER FOUR

he skies have opened and the rain is pouring down, but Mathieu doesn't care. He walks through it, getting drenched by the sheets of rain that don't appear to be letting up anytime soon. Mathieu zips up his dark jacket and flips the hood over his head. His goal is not to shield the elements of weather but rather to conceal his identity. He pulls it tight to cover his face and thinks to himself that this is the price of fame.

He revels in the drama of this moment.

At this hour in the night, he probably looks like a bank robber or a thief ready to snatch up jewels and electronics, but as long as he doesn't look like Mathieu Deneuve, he does not care. Plus, there is no one out in Madeleine's neighborhood. If there are, they are peeping through their windows, and that is just as sketchy, he thinks.

Madeleine is his twin sister, and he has a key to her apartment. He knows she won't mind, so he lets himself in, since she isn't even there. She probably won't even know about his sneaky visit. She is in Prague shooting her first big feature film. Like Mathieu, they are both artistic. However, Mathieu prefers to be center stage—well, usually, at least—while Madeleine prefers to be behind the scenes as a director.

The last thing Mathieu wants is for anyone to recognize him or for the cops to be called for a suspicious-person alert, so he takes extra precautions to make sure he isn't seen by waiting for the coast to clear before entering the building's main door. To his luck, a neighbor's dog starts barking out of a ground floor window—at him.

"Hush, little guy," Mathieu whispers. Again, loving the drama of the scene, he quickly inserts the key into the back door, letting himself in. The dog still hasn't stopped barking, and as Mathieu slips inside the building, he hears the owner telling the dog to be quiet.

I made it! he thinks, locking the door behind him.

He wipes water from his face, drenched from the downpour, and he fumbles along the wall, trying to find the light switch. When he turns the light on, his eyes sting for minute in the brightness.

He is alone.

He pauses and lets that sink in.

No bandmates, no paparazzi, no managers, no fans, no record executives, no one nagging him.

He's alone for the first time in what feels like forever.

"Yes!" Mathieu shouts out to no one in particular.

He's done it! He has really done it. He has escaped. No one knows where he is, and they certainly don't know where to find him, which is more than fine with him. Morning will be here before he knows it, but for tonight, he is a normal, average guy in a normal, average apartment, doing normal, average things that can't be done on tour buses and hotels...like taking a bath.

Sometimes a man just wants to get clean. Baths didn't happen on tour buses and in crappy hotels. Feeling free and high at this very thought of being ordinary, Mathieu strikes a couple chords on an imaginary air guitar, sticking to the B, E, and A notes. He continues jamming out and dancing, all the way upstairs. Mathieu is so into his dancing and jam session that he misses a step and tumbles to the floor, banging his knee.

He groans in pain, and his knee is throbbing, but he bounces back up and continues playing on his air guitar, adding in the D and E notes this time. There isn't a particular tune on his mind, just the stringing together of chords, how music is made he thinks, and Mathieu only stops to turn the water spout on and plug the drain in the giant tub in the master bathroom.

He strips off his drenched clothes. The rain was so torrential that it has soaked him entirely, and he literally has to peel his pants and shirt off, as if he were taking a Band-Aid off his body, peeling slowly at the corners. He raises his left foot, dunks it in the water.

Fully immersed now, he lets out a deep breath, a sigh of exhaustion, not realizing just how tired his bones and muscles had become.

He lets himself just sit and soak. He closes his eyes and tries to clear his mind of everything that is on it, the band, the note, and the not knowing what he is going to do next. Quite frankly, Mathieu doesn't even care at this moment what tomorrow will bring. Tonight, he feels like a real human, not a musical puppet.

Stretched out, submerged in the water, Mathieu tries to recall the last time that he heard just silence. The silence is so unfamiliar that it almost pierces his eardrum.

Just as he has that very thought, his cell phone rings from his pants pocket and he reaches his hand out to try to grab the pants leg closer so he doesn't have to get out of the bath. Unfortunately, it's out of reach and the sound of the bleeping phone is irritating him, so he sighs with frustration and gets out of the bath. Just as he is reaching for it in the pocket, it stops, which irritates him further.

As if it were possible, Mathieu's irritation reaches a new level of annoyance when he sees the missed call is from Adrien Henri, the record executive for Les Slinks. Adrien Henri is an overweight man who hides his pudge by wearing designer clothes. Clothes can only go so far in Mathieu's opinion, which was made quite clear when, during a magazine interview, Mathieu described Adrien as a "balding, ruddy-faced man, with unsavory character."

The reporter just happened to catch Mathieu when he was in a contagiously wild mood, pulling out another gem of a quote when Mathieu proudly shared that all of Les Slinks' band members referred to Adrien as *He Who Shall Not Be Named*, a Harry Potter reference.

Once published, that article didn't go over so well with Adrien or with Mathieu's mother. Mama Deneuve threatened to wash his mouth out with soap, not caring that he was an adult.

Yet they were interdependent on one another. While Mathieu and Adrien had a tendency to clash heads often, Adrien Henri needed Les Slinks on his label and Les Slinks needed a label that allowed creativity and freedom in the studio.

Realizing he has just been standing naked in the bathroom and brooding over his bath interruption, Mathieu notices a handful of text messages and voicemails that he must have missed. If only their old band manager, Jacque, still worked for them. He was usually the one whole who dealt with issues within the band and with the label. Jacque bailed when his wife gave birth to twin girls, understandably, but now Les Slinks are without a manager.

"Well, I'm already out now," Mathieu mutters.

He opens up the linen closet in the bathroom and pulls out a plush pink towel. First a bath and now a pink towel. If his bandmates saw him, they would never let him live it down.

First time for everything, he thinks, wrapping the towel around him and ignoring the pile of clothes strewn on the floor.

"I'll deal with this tomorrow," Mathieu mutters at his cell phone.

He grabs his clothes, opens the dryer door, shoves all his clothes in, and turns them to a quick dry cycle.

From there, it's straight to the kitchen. He opens up the fridge and the pantry. To his dismay, it's fairly empty since Madeleine is out of town, but he manages to find a package of supermarket-bought madeleines, some Camembert cheese, and a green apple.

"This'll have to work," Mathieu says out loud, again to no one, and sits on the kitchen counter to devour his snacks. It's been awhile since he has last eaten, and his irritation of Adrien Henri melts away after the first couple of bites.

As if he couldn't have timed it any better, he hears the buzz of the dryer go off, indicating his clothes should be dry. He pulls them out, puts them back on, and feels like a kid again. On cold winter nights, his mom would stick all their pajamas in the dryer for just a few minutes, and when they came out, they would all be warm and toasty. Wearing warm pajamas is equivalent to eating a giant marshmallow toasted over a crackling fire.

Mathieu stifles a yawn and quickly falls asleep

He awakes the next morning to see that it's after eleven. He is greeted with a headache, not the type that is totally debilitating, but rather, the type that makes completing the simplest tasks just slightly more difficult and annoying. Like the fact that it takes Mathieu a solid couple of minutes to figure out where he is and what happened the night before. Slowly he pieces it all back together.

The note.

He remembers handing his drummer the note.

For a moment shorter than it takes to blink an eye, Mathieu feels a pang of regret, a what-did-I-do kind of feeling.

The truth is, Mathieu isn't remorseful about this. There are plenty of things he is regretful about in his life. But this is not one of them.

He doesn't even feel remotely sorry when he sees that his voicemail and text messages have reached their capacity.

He makes the giant mistake of looking at his social media pages, where fans are speculating where Mathieu was when he missed a few television appearances and the band couldn't perform and only ended up doing interviews.

"Oh geez," he mutters while realizing that there are conspiracy theories in less than twenty-four hours after his so-called disappearance.

The label has had to do some damage control.

Adrien Henri and company released an official statement addressing the rumors that Mathieu Deneuve had quit the band. They just got off tour and are enjoying some much needed time off and so on and so forth.

At least Adrien squelched the story, as if it were a spider being stomped on the kitchen floor, and for that, Mathieu is grateful. Dare he even say, appreciative? No, that would be taking things too far. Mathieu hates Adrien, but in this instance, the record exec is on his side, even though Adrien is more likely protecting his own image.

A label exec who can't find his lead singer? Admitting that would make Adrien the laughingstock of the French music industry...again!

Okay, Mathieu does feel a little sorry for what he's done. Sooner or later, he's going to have to face the music.

At that thought, he lets out a sigh of annoyance. As if on cue, someone knocks on the door. Mathieu stays still; he has no intentions of opening it.

Whoever is there knocks two more times. Bang, bang, he hears against the wooden door.

Having a hangover and headache and simply not caring, Mathieu puts the pillow over his face and falls right back into deep sleep.

Much later that afternoon, Mathieu wakes up and is both groggy and refreshed at the same time. Groggy from the long hibernation nap and refreshed because he has an idea. His little refuge to Madeleine's place has been so relaxing, and he is full of creative ideas now. He wants nothing more than to grab a pad of paper and pour his soul out in the form of lyrics. But not just any lyrics; Mathieu wants the lyrics to be fresh, new, and authentic.

He knows his passion is music—it's not even a question. However, the industry has been dictating too much of Les Slinks' direction, something none of what the band wanted. Like their album in English. Mathieu didn't even get to write the songs, because he only writes in French.

Les Slinks should be unique; they should have their own flavor. Their music and their rules had lately been turning into Adrien Henri's rules and formulaic, predictable songs. They reminded him of songs that would be sung and performed by one-hit wonders, which was not Les Slinks.

All Mathieu knows is this: his creativity has been amplified at Madeleine's place. All he needs to do is escape and spend some more time alone. He needs his own retreat, his own house, where he can return to his artistic roots and feel more grounded.

"I'm buying a house!" Mathieu says aloud to himself with exuberance, pulling himself out of the bed.

He, Mathieu Deneuve, is buying a house all for himself. Perhaps he'll call it Chateau Deneuve or the Maison de Mathieu. He'll be so famous one day that when he dies, they'll turn his home into a museum and tourists will come to visit. *It'll be just like Elvis and Graceland*, he thinks, laughing at the very thought.

CHAPTER FIVE

After his night and day of sleeping, Mathieu is starving for a real meal. Last night's snack wore off a long time ago, so he is rummaging through Madeleine's cupboards once again. He opens a drawer—her junk drawer. Sorting through the papers, scissors, tape, coupons, and spare keys, he's about to close it.

But something catches his eye. Lying right there, on the top of the stack, is a pile of business cards. Mathieu cannot believe his luck when he sees the card for Domaines D'Elegance, a real estate company. The name sounds familiar. Then he remembers that this is the company that Madeleine has used for a movie shoot. She used to scout locations for films before working her way up to the director's chair. For a prior movie, they helped her locate a mansion to use for shooting or something like that.

Mathieu stares at the card in disbelief and thinks, *How much more of a sign can this be? It's destiny.*

His own house, a sanctuary. He feels anxious and excited, and so much positivity is flowing through this veins.

"It's fate! It has to be," Mathieu exclaims jubilantly.

Yes, yes, yes! Mathieu plays his guitar in excitement once again and feels music bringing him back to life, even through the silly imaginary action.

Without wasting another second, Mathieu deletes all of the voicemails and all of the text messages from his cell phone and hastily dials the number on the card.

It rings once.

It rings twice.

On the third ring, he hears a click and then a voice. "Hello, thank you for calling Domaines D'Elegance. My name is Brigitte, how can I be of assistance today?"

"Hi, Brigitte," Mathieu says, feeling a little nervous all of the sudden. "I am interested in buying a home outside of Paris, and I'm wondering what I need to do to get started in my search."

"Wonderful news!" Brigitte says. "If you have a few minutes now, I just need to know a little bit about what you are looking for, and then we can schedule you an appointment with one of our Domaines D'Elegance realtors."

"Yes, now is fine, thank you, Brigitte," Mathieu says.

"Lovely, what is your name, sir?" she asks.

"Mat–" he says, pausing before he continues.

"I'm sorry, I didn't catch that."

Obviously he can't say his first name, as that will blow his cover, so he fudges just a little. His mood changes again. This time, he is moody because of the receptionist's question. Being off the grid is harder than he thought.

"It's Luc," Mathieu says. "Luc Deneuve."

"All right, thank you very much, Luc. Now, can you tell me a little bit about the style of home you are looking for? Apartment? High-rise? Neighborhood? For how many people?"

"Oh, man, so many choices, er, um," Mathieu stutters because he isn't really sure, so he describes a house similar to his childhood home in Montmartre. "I'm looking for a single-family home, it doesn't have to be huge or anything. I am looking for space and privacy, and I do not want it to be in Paris or in a really crowded suburb of Paris."

"All right, sir, and do you have a preference for realtor?" Brigitte asks him.

"No, just somebody who can meet me tomorrow. Is that too soon?" he says.

"We work around your schedule, Mr. Deneuve. Tomorrow afternoon, let's see... Violette Deschamps is available, and she is currently accepting clients. How does eleven a.m. work for you, sir?"

"Just Luc is fine, and I can meet then. Oh, and I did just want to let you know that your company comes with the highest recommendation from Madeleine Deneuve."

"Madeleine Deneuve? Are you perhaps related?"

"I'm her brother," Mathieu says. "Well, one of them."

"Madeleine is a local celebrity at this office! We just loved working with her. How exciting that you are her brother."

Mathieu flinches at the word *celebrity*, but he kind of likes seeing someone fawn over a different Deneuve than him.

"Yeah, she's pretty great, she is..." Mathieu pauses, about to stay she is his twin. "She is really talented," he says instead.

"She is," Brigitte agrees with genuine enthusiasm. "Is there anything else I can do for you?"

"There is one thing. Could you keep it in your discretion that I will be working with your company? I don't want to draw attention to myself or the fact that I'm Madeleine's sibling," Mathieu says, trying to conceal his own identity in a roundabout way.

"Of course. Well, Mr. Luc Deneuve, I have you down for eleven a.m. tomorrow. Meet Violette Deschamps at the bistro beside the Domaines D'Elegance office. Have a nice day!"

Feeling proud of his decision, Mathieu just knows this is the first step to turning his life around. It's time for him finally to get his ideas on track with reality. He can't wait to get back to his musical roots, not the trite work that Adrien Henri wants Les Slinks to play. Just thinking about Adrien makes Mathieu shudder, but he tries not to dwell on this, as the second step to turning his life around is getting some food. Knowing he can't just walk out of here unnoticed, he once again gets agitated.

Madeleine's closet is a mess, but he sorts through a pile of her accessories and pulls out a black cap. He throws his own hooded jacket on and walks out of the apartment.

"Okay, Mathieu, just do it. Act calm, act normal," he says to himself as he approaches the neighborhood supermarket.

The automatic doors open for him, and he enters, grateful that it is not crowded. He grabs a shopping cart and starts at the produce section, grabbing avocados and apples, happy that no one is paying him any attention. Before he knows it, he is on the other side of the grocery store with enough food to last him at least a week, probably much longer.

He stops at the beer, wine, and liquor section and pauses. He almost doesn't get anything, but knowing he wants to make as few trips out as possible, he grabs a few bottles of liquor and a case of beer.

Just because he buys it, doesn't mean he has to drink, Mathieu reasons. He tells himself that if he buys it, he will, under no circumstances, drink tonight since he wants to make sure he is clear for his meeting with the realtor tomorrow.

Dilemma solved, Mathieu heads to the check out and sees there are two lines available, both with one person ahead of him. He chooses the line where an elderly man is ringing up a young mom at a rate so slow it's almost funny. Despite the snail-speed cashier, Mathieu reasons that it's a safer choice than the other line, where a girl, probably in her teens, is ringing up a different customer. He hopes she'll slow down just a little bit, so he isn't called over to her register.

Old guy is finishing up, but not quickly enough.

"C'mon, c'mon," he whispers.

It's finally his turn, and he starts putting his items on the register beltway.

"How are you doing today, young man?" the cashier asks in a grandfatherly tone.

"Good, you?" Mathieu says, trying to speak as little as possible.

"Good, good, just another day," he says. "Say, you look familiar. You come here often, don't you?"

Mathieu panics on the inside, fearing his cover being blown.

"No, I'm visiting friends, so I'm not very familiar with the area at all." Mathieu fears he's being more verbose than he should be.

The man finishes ringing up the last item, and Mathieu pays in cash.

Just as Mathieu finishes bagging his purchases, the older gentleman says, "Well, I know I have seen you before, and you look awfully familiar, but these old eyes are always playing tricks on me. Have yourself a good evening!"

With that, Mathieu is free. He did it, just barely perhaps, but he did it. Carrying half a dozen bags of groceries, he wishes he'd brought Madeleine's shopping buggy. He feels a jolt of fear when he passes other people on the street, afraid someone will recognize him and stop him.

When he gets back to Madeleine's place, he unpacks his groceries and starts making dinner. He sautés an onion for the marinara sauce, and just the smell of the onion cooking, of real home cooking, makes him feel more at ease already.

He decides that one small drink won't hurt him. One drink is fine, normal, and socially acceptable, he reasons.

He adds the tomato sauce and Italian spices to the pan and pours another drink. He stirs the marinara and takes a swig of beer. Mathieu enjoys every drop of the beer taste going down his throat, with its hint of cider, malt base, and a rich, sticky sort of sweet taste.

He adds pasta to boiling water and grabs another beer from the fridge. He counts the bottles in the trash. One. Two. Three.

This will be his last. Lucky number four, and then once again, he reasons with himself—he is done drinking for tonight.

The timer beeps for the pasta, and he finds a colander to drain the noodles. He scoops a handful of the pasta into a bowl and ladles a spoonful of fresh homemade sauce right in the middle. He takes his freshly cooked dinner into the living room to watch TV.

After dinner, he has one more drink, a nightcap, for dessert, and figures he already broke this promise to himself, to his new life. Feeling irate, he continues to drink and plows through beer after beer. He doesn't pay attention to what is on the television, and he gets lost in his own thoughts of inferiority, fame, failure, and success.

Mathieu recognizes that he is drunk, and he is furious. He isn't supposed to be doing this. He is supposed to be clearheaded, and yet here he lies on the floor, too exhausted to crawl onto the couch, feeling more temperamental than ever before.

He takes one last swig and falls into a deep, deep sleep where he dreams of fighting with his bandmates.

Even in his nightmares, he's trying to figure out his next move.

CHAPTER SIX

*M*athieu wakes up, his eyes burning from the light coming in through the blinds. His back and neck are stiff from sleeping on the hard floor all night, but he has to get up and start moving if he wants to make it to his appointment at Domaines D'Elegance. He sits up slowly, scratching his eyes, and knowing with a bad feeling in his stomach that he looks terrible. This hangover is much worse than the previous ones he's had.

Crap.

This one is the hangover that Olivier named the what-have-I-done hangover, the hangover where you can't quite remember what you did or said, but you know it was wrong, and you are littered with both paranoia and self-loathing. Mathieu is thankful he was alone, but he feels so much shame, especially because this is supposed to be his beginning, his fresh start.

Mathieu swears out loud, wishing that he could hit a reset button for yesterday.

Once again he promises himself that he has to do better.

"I am not going to drink today," he says. "Not even a sip."

Growing up, when all the Deneuve kids were getting ready for school, Audrey and Madeleine would often forget to turn off the hair straightener, and so their mom came up with this little mnemonic device. She said that if you say out loud that you will turn off the hair straightener, turn off the oven, etc., that you will remember that you did or you will remember to avoid something. Mathieu sure hoped it worked with drinking, so he repeats his new mantra.

"I am not going to drink today, not even a sip."

Realizing that he can't go to the meeting with realtor looking like this, Mathieu quickly showers, puts on his dirty clothes, and has no choice but to stop somewhere and pick up a few new items. To try to minimize his time in any store, he looks online at his favorite store, calls, and asks to speak with the manager.

"Auguste, this is Mathieu, I need a favor, and I need you to be extremely discreet. Please, please, don't tell anyone about this phone call."

Mathieu is a huge customer and has generated a significant sales boost to the store. The store even sponsors the band members at some of Les Slinks' events.

"Of course, I won't say a word," Auguste says. "What do you need?"

"I'm coming by in about thirty minutes. I will park out front, and I want you to bring me a mix of distressed jeans and T-shirts. You know my size and style. Let's say three pairs of pants and six shirts," Mathieu says, feeling as though he is ordering food at a drive-thru window. "Also, I need to give you a different card than the one you have on file."

"All right, but, Mathieu, may I ask what's going on?" Auguste asks.

"I just need some space right now. It is that simple," Mathieu answers, knowing that it's the truth, but a complicated truth. "Can you help me? Please, Auguste?"

"I won't say a word. Go ahead and give me your card number, and I will have a bag ready for you when you pull up," Auguste says.

"Hang on just a second," Mathieu says. He flips open his brown leather wallet and grabs his black debit card, a card for a personal spending account that he keeps private and for emergencies.

Mathieu declares this as an emergency. In his dramatic world, this is the equivalent of a tornado ripping through a venue right before taking stage or a rare snowstorm that leaves him stranded on an autoroute, miles from the nearest town.

"See ya, Auguste, and remember, not a word to anyone," Mathieu says before hanging up.

With a sigh of relief, Mathieu is glad that was easier than he thought it would be. He grabs a quick bowl of cereal, hails a cab, and heads to pick up his clothes. He still feels the hangover curse looming over him, but at least he is off to a decent start today.

He pulls up to the front of Auguste's shop and asks the cab driver to beep a couple of times, alerting Auguste of his arrival. He waits a moment, but when Auguste doesn't come out, Mathieu sighs in irritation.

"Please wait here. I'll be right back, sir," Mathieu says to the driver and jumps out of the car. With speed comparable to that of a cheetah in the African wilds, Mathieu dashes into the small store, quickly finds Auguste, grabs his bag full of clothes, and slides back into the backseat of the taxi.

When he gets back into the cab, the cab driver turns to show his face. With a feeling of instant disdain and a pit in his stomach, Mathieu realizes with horror that the cab driver, who he called sir, is actually a husky woman.

Mathieu says a silent prayer to whatever spirits might be above that maybe, just maybe, this taxi driver didn't hear him call her sir, and he proceeds to share the address of the bistro.

Earlier that morning

Violette wakes up early, as usual, and wishes she could go back to sleep. The alarm clock is one of the most dreadful inventions ever. It is ranked right up there with the bra. Still foggy from her night's sleep, her feet hit the floor of her comfortable, tidy apartment. She instinctively makes her bed, a habit she has done since she was a young girl and later reinforced by a speech she was saw on the Internet, saying that by making the bed in the morning, you will be much more successful during the day.

She strolls into her bathroom and takes a shower. When she gets out, she stands in front of her closet, trying to figure out what to wear. Since she is meeting a new client, she plans to dress up a little and pulls out a pretty floral frock with a tiny print of blue and yellow flowers. It's one of her favorites, although well worn. She grabs a pair of flats that matches the dress, and she gives herself a once-over glance in the full-length mirror. She thinks to herself that this will do just fine. She grabs her morning coffee and a light breakfast. Before she knows it, she is strolling through the classy front doors of Domaines D'Elegance.

As soon as she walks in, Jean-Philippe is pouncing on her with big news.

"Violette!" he says with great enthusiasm.

"Jean-Philippe, if this is about your nephew, I said I would think about it," Violette says.

"No, this is about your client," he says.

"What client?" Violette asks. "A new client?"

"His name is Luc Deneuve," Jean-Philippe says, emphasizing the name Deneuve.

Not missing a beat, Violette says, "Deneuve? Any relation to Madeleine Deneuve?"

"Yes, it's her brother. He has requested discretion with this case. He doesn't want to be fussed over, and so you are to treat him as if he is any other client while understanding that he is more than just any other client. I did a search on the Internet, and it turns out that Luc is very successful. He owns LUX, a huge advertising agency. Luc gets the royal treatment without knowing he is getting the royal treatment, if you get what I'm saying." Jean-Philippe ends his monologue and claps his hands together in front of his waist. "Oh dear."

"Now what?" Violette says, feeling amused by all of this hoopla.

"How do I say this nicely, Violette?" Jean-Philippe pauses and raises his eyebrows at her. "It's just that we need to spruce up your look. We need to give you an edge. You're sweet and beautiful, but we need modern, fun, edgy, ultraprofessional. You remember how trendy Madeleine is. Luc would also be dressed in the best clothes."

Violette's cheeks flush; she is not sure how to take this. She isn't used to being ordered around, let alone ordered to change her clothes.

"Please don't take offense, sweetheart," Jean-Philippe says, looking sheepish, almost regretful that he said anything. "You are wonderful as is—you know I think that—but this is just a business transaction."

"No, it's okay," Violette says, brushing off the fire of pure embarrassment that is blazing like a wildfire deep within her soul. "I get it."

It's not personal; it's business, Violette hears a little tiny voice inside her head saying.

"You're mad, aren't you?"

"Nope," she says, shrugging her shoulders nonchalantly.

"Here is what is going to happen. You will go back to your place, change, and meet your client. Do you want Brigitte to go with you?"

"I'd be happy to," the perky receptionist adds. "I love makeovers! I'll make you look like a model."

"But I need to finish preparing my potential house list," Violette starts to argue, although she know that Jean-Philippe won't negotiate on this. "And, no, I don't need your help, Brigitte, but thanks." Brigitte's comment has made her feel even frumpier.

Unfortunately, once Jean-Philippe makes up his mind, there is no stopping him.

"I've already started working on it. It will be ready by the time you get back. Now, time's wasting. Go!"

Violette knows she must follow in suit. Like a dog being told to sit, Violette heads out the door, obeying her orders.

En route to her place, she sits in a traffic jam.

"This isn't happening to me," Violette cries and gently rests her head on the steering wheel.

She doesn't have time for this and she hates the idea of being late to any meeting, let alone a first client meeting. Violette decides to do a little bit of creative driving to get out of the cars that are barely moving amidst all the traffic commotion.

When she gets to a roundabout, she takes a different turn than normal and puts pressure on the gas pedal to speed up her little car. *Go, go, go!*

When she gets to her home, finally, she is racing against the clock.

Violette quickly rummages through her closet for the second time today and pulls out a business suit she rarely wears. She prefers the more casual, or business casual, look. She wears an emerald-green shirt underneath it, which brings out the color in her eyes. She switches out her funky earrings for her pearls, and looks through her modest-sized shoe collection. Unfortunately, flats are not an option, and she reaches for a pair of heels that elongate her legs while slowly murdering her feet with great brutality.

As much as she hates high heels, she knows this is one occasion where she must suffer through and wear them. On second thought, she grabs a pair of flats that matches her suit and throws them in her purse, knowing she will change into them the minute that her meeting with Luc Deneuve is over. She gives herself one more full-mirror view, and she's pleasantly surprised with the outcome. After adding a dab of glossy pink lip gloss and running a comb through her hair, Violette smiles to herself.

"Perfect!" she says out loud.

Wasting not even a second more, Violette sprints back to her car and speeds away from her Parisian suburb and back to the beloved city limits.

What a morning! An ordinary day has warped into one of many peculiarities, and when she nervously glances at her watch, she knows that she will be late to her meeting. Unfortunately for the girl who always loves to be on time to everything, being punctual is just not an option for today. Violette has a tendency to show up chronically early to wherever she needs to be.

It's both a blessing and a curse, she muses, as she turns up the radio.

By the time she arrives at the front step of Domaines D'Elegance, she is officially nine minutes late to her meeting. She called Jean-Philippe from her cell phone and asked if he could have the listings pulled up on her laptop. He did that and has her computer ready waiting for her at Brigitte's desk, the first thing you see when you come in the front door.

As soon as Brigitte sees Violette, she meets her in the middle with the laptop. They usher in quick hellos and good-byes, and Violette makes it to the door of the bistro precisely eleven minutes after the agreed-upon time.

So much for a punctual first impression, Violette thinks, letting herself catch her breath before pushing open the bistro doors.

All right, Violette, it's show time. She walks into the bistro feigning an air of great confidence.

CHAPTER SEVEN

*I*t is before the lunchtime rush, so the quintessential French bistro isn't terribly crowded yet. Violette scans the place and sees two potential "Luc Deneuves" in the restaurant. The question is which one she should approach. She knows she needs to make a split-second decision.

Option number one is a heavyset man dressed in khaki pants and a white oxford shirt. He is clean cut and probably works in business. The other is a younger guy, handsome, in a graphic T-shirt; he's a little disheveled.

She chooses Khaki Pants Man. She approaches his table, and when he looks up from reading the paper, she cheerfully says, "Hi, Luc."

He shakes his head no and jokes that she can sit down and have lunch with him anyway. As he is talking, Distressed Jeans Man looks over at her and seems particularly annoyed. He gives her a little wave, putting two fingers in the air and giving a little nod with his head.

First impression? Violette is instantly struck by his good looks.

He has an edgy, urban look, and she notices a tattoo on his left shoulder. She can't make out what the tattoo is—only that he has one. Violette looks away. She stifles a blush and instead tries to focus on the fact that he is sending off vibes of pompousness with the big old scowl on his face.

Egotistical clients are the worst to deal with since they are self-righteous and act as though they are entitled to the world. And whatever happened to Luc Deneuve being a stylish dresser?

Fake smiling, she walks across the restaurant to greet the real Luc Deneuve.

"Hi, I'm Violette Deschamps from Domaines D'Elegance. You must be Mr. Deneuve, I presume?"

"Just call me Luc, please," he says in a chilly tone.

"I'm terribly sorry for being so late," she says. "I got caught up. I promise it's not my usual pattern."

Mathieu's mind is reeling with negativity, but he won't deny that Violette Deschamps is pretty in a singular kind of way. She has a classic face, nothing necessarily extraordinary: nice brown eyes, dark blond hair, and soft lips.

There is something unique about her–that much he can tell–but probably just because he is used to all the fan girls with skimpy clothes and flirty attitudes.

Violette is far from those types of girls. Here she stands in front of him looking uncomfortable but confident. Her face shows a look of determination, while the rest of her just looks intolerable and twitchy in an ill-fitting suit. He senses she doesn't really have much style, and he guesses that there are approximately zero items in her closet and dressers that resemble anything with a designer label.

For style, he rates her at a two out of ten.

For punctuality, she gets a gigantic zero. What kind of professional is ten minutes late to a critical meeting? And how dare she make him just sit here in pure misery. Her excuse was lamer than he imagined it would be.

The fact that he is nursing a hangover complete with a pounding headache in the bright sunlight-filled bistro doesn't help. Mathieu feels as though he is a victim here, a victim of Violette's poor time management.

His enthusiasm for the house hunting dwindles, as he wasn't really expecting it to get off to such a rocky start, but he decides to make the best of it.

"Have a seat," Mathieu decides not to say a word about Violette's lack of promptness.

"Thanks, and again, I'm really sorry, Luc," Violette says, making a mental note that this guy is a jerk and to take extra precautions to be early next time—if there is a next time.

She also silently curses Jean-Philippe for making her late.

Sensing that he isn't one for small talk, Violette dives right into the pool of business. When she opens her laptop, the waitress comes over. Violette orders a green tea with an almond croissant and asks if Luc wants anything, indicating that it's her treat.

Rather coarsely, he declines, and she wills herself not to roll her eyes.

She pulls up her list of properties and turns the laptop toward Luc so he can see them easily.

"Brigitte gave me your client profile," Violette says, "and I have put together a long list of potential homes that will work based on that conversation."

"I told Brigitte that I wanted to look at houses as soon as possible," he says flatly. "I'm ready to buy now."

"I certainly understand that." Violette takes a sip of tea after the waitress gives it to her. It is much hotter than she expects.

The burning sensation makes her wince, and for a moment, Mathieu is caught off guard by her cute expression.

He can't resist but lets out a half-smile.

"Hot?" he asks.

"Very," Violette says, locking eyes with him for just a moment and returning the smile, before looking away. "So, yes, I am aware that you would like to tour potential listings as soon as possible. Since you have broad requirements, I thought in today's meeting we could narrow down a few properties that you would like to see. I don't want to waste your time dragging you to properties that aren't of interest. We will go through some of these, and I'll jot down notes, get a better feel for your price point, style, and such. Will that work?"

"Yes," Mathieu says, although he thinks this is a waste of time.

If he wanted to look at properties online, he could have saved himself the trouble of finding clothes and sitting in this bistro full of sunshine and brightness that is making his head pound.

Anytime this woman talks, Mathieu's head just throbs with a thudding violence, kind of as if he were slamming his head into a wall repeatedly.

"And please, give me honest feedback as we look at these," Violette says, hoping to encourage more than one-word answers from this guy, who she can't quite figure out. "Let's start with this one."

She shows Luc a charming property that looks like a cottage-size castle. Off-white stucco exterior, elongated windows, lots of extras on the outside, surrounded by trees.

"I hate it," Mathieu says nonchalantly.

"Okay," Violette says slowly. "Can you be a little more specific? Do you want to look at the inside photos?"

"Why would I want to look at the inside of a house that looks dreadful on the outside?" he says with a tone of mockery.

"Moving along then." She clicks the red X to close the page.

The next property that Violette pulls up is a quaint oasis that looks like a Tuscan cottage. It is very different from the first choice—funky roof lines, a long porch at the front of the house, covered in red mossy flowers, a mix of tan and off-white stucco, complete with a pathway to the house surrounded by well-maintained flowers in bright, beautiful hues of yellows. There is even a teal-colored shutter on the front of the house.

Violette thinks its charm is something of a children's book, where magic lives and stories come to life, which is why she fully expects an instant rejection from Luc.

"Better," Mathieu says, raising his hand for the waitress to come take his order.

Violette is shocked—something positive from this guy? Perhaps there is hope.

When the waitress arrives, he orders a black coffee and a croissant, the same type as Violette's, which doubly surprises her.

She begins clicking through the property, but her burst of hope is quickly deadened when Luc says absolutely nothing positive about the inside of this home. The kitchen is too small, the bathroom needs remodeling, the walls need to be repainted, and there's too much sunlight in the bedroom.

Some are normal complaints, but who complains about too much natural light? Violette wills herself not to say anything.

He eats his croissant, a few crumbs sticking to his face, which Violette guesses hasn't been shaved in at least two days. She considers saying something, but warns herself not to.

As he is eating, Violette shows him property after property, providing just one or two words of feedback. Nothing seems to be good enough. Violette can't even zone in on the style that he wants and what he doesn't like. There seems to be no pattern, no direction in what Luc Deneuve wants.

Could he be any more lackadaisical? Violette tries not to let her growing annoyance show.

Finally, she can't take it anymore. She wants to walk away from this deal, but she doesn't want to subject anyone else at Domaines D'Elegance to this nonsensical waste of time. Yes, she thinks he is good looking, but good looks can only get you so far.

As they are clicking through the long list Jean-Philippe put together, Violette decides to take a new approach with Luc. She can't take much more of this spoiled-brat behavior from a grown man. To say she is over it is an understatement.

"Luc, I am here to help you. I am here to help make *your* transition to *your* house a smooth one. However, how comfortable this transaction is, is up to you and your behavior. Now, I would love the opportunity to help you. Please know that I am not a mind reader nor am I here to wave my nonexistent magic wand. I can't say, 'abracadabra,' and a house that you will love just magically appears. If I understand what you are looking for, then the chances of us finding your perfect home will greatly increase. I think we have seen enough for today. Please call me when you are ready to take this seriously." Violette says all of this in a kind, but firm manner.

She starts gathering her belongings as if she is going to leave and waits for a response from Luc, who she notices is looking a little stunned.

Mathieu, on the other side of the table is feeling rather stunned. No one ever calls him out. He's used to making the shots for Les Slinks and his life, and he lets himself admit that Violette surprised him. She has more gumption than he originally thought. He kind of likes it, and he doesn't really want her to leave just yet.

"Okay, I'm sorry," Mathieu says, unable to stop the apology from tumbling out. He makes a mental note to himself to be more involved and to stop being a jerk.

"No apologies are necessary," Violette says, feeling pleased that he has responded positively to her monologue, which she worried sounded like the scolding of a small child in primary school.

"I liked the Tuscan-inspired cottage," he says, offering a peacemaking smile to Violette.

Violette feels the tension in her stomach release. He does have a nice smile.

"Now we are getting somewhere," Violette says, offering a small grin back.

Mathieu notices that the smile lights up her entire face. She looks softer, lovelier.

Violette shows Mathieu three more properties, and the two make a list of properties to visit and tour.

"At your convenience, I will schedule these appointments." She hands him a business card with a website on the back. "At your leisure, feel free to take a look at this site. It has all the available properties, pictures, and information about the available homes. If you see any you would like to visit, just let me know."

"Thank you, Violette," Mathieu says, feeling sheepish of his previous behavior. "I'll be in touch."

As Violette makes her exit from the bistro and their meeting, Mathieu finds himself watching her. He notices that even in the ill-fitting suit, Miss Violette Deschamps has a shapely body with curves he didn't notice at first.

He realizes that he is genuinely looking forward to seeing the houses, and not just to find his new home. He can't wait to see this woman again and more importantly, he can't believe how much his mood has improved over their conversation.

His attraction to her takes him by surprise. What is it about her that's so different from the women he usually meets?

Maybe it's that she leads with her intelligence rather than her beauty. As uncomfortable as she looks in her clothes, she has a certain boldness about her. She's blunt and gets to the point. But he can also tell she has warmth and a lot of heart.

The combination of those things has a peculiar effect on him. The more he thinks about her, the more she drives him wild.

As he walks out of the bistro, he realizes one more thing about her that endears him.

Violette exudes a silent vulnerability that makes him want to take care of her.

CHAPTER EIGHT

*A*drien Henri sits in his office in a stupor. It has been a few days since he has seen Mathieu Deneuve, and none of the other band members have heard from him. No text, no e-mail, no phone call.

Adrien even took it upon himself to call local hospitals to see if Mathieu was sick or injured. He even went so far as to ask one of the hospitals if there were any male patients without an identity. Sadly, there were not.

After the calls to the hospital, Adrien turned to the police stations. He used his connections to see if anyone named Mathieu Deneuve was in prison. He scoured the recent police records for any hint or sign that they had come across anything related to his disappearance. He actually tried to put in a case for Mathieu as a missing-persons case, but it was denied since he had handed them a note before fleeing the VIP lounge just nights before.

Mathieu's disappearance has been a total nightmare for Adrien and his entire label. As the record executive, this is bad public relations for his brand, the entire Les Slinks band, and for Adrien personally. He has big plans for Les Slinks, and by big plans for Les Slinks, he means he has big plans for himself. More specifically, the success of Les Slinks is his ticket to purchasing a house in the south of France, overlooking the Mediterranean coast.

Now, all of that is in dire jeopardy thanks to Mathieu Deneuve. Adrien is the type of man who thinks he is owed something by the universe, a special little snowflake, one of a kind. He feels as if he deserves some lavish lifestyle that should be bestowed upon him like a crown of jewels presented to a royal princess in a fairy tale. He knows the music industry, he has been working in it for a long time, and Les Slinks is how he plans to make it big. They are known around the world, and he had just been about to dive into an Olympic-size pool of money before this trouble started.

Adrien stands up from the beautiful mahogany desk with inlaid, ornate carvings and starts walking around his small office, running his hands along the spines of the binders and books sitting neatly on the bookcases.

The money, Adrien thinks, will change him. It will give him more power, a fancier life, and he feels as though his one chance might slip right through his fingers because of Mathieu. As he sits at his desk, he shakes his fists in anger, not sure exactly what his next strategic move is going be. He feels as if he is playing an intense championship game of chess—one wrong move and it's game over.

But Adrien Henri is not one to get rolled over by some edgy rock star, which is why he has to come up with a plan. He is pacing back and forth, something he does when he thinks, racking his brain for a solution, a plan of attack.

In just the few days of the dramatic disappearance of the band's lead singer, Adrien has had to cancel not one, not two, but three major television appearances and for no good excuse. This is a giant deal in the music industry world.

Not to mention, Les Slinks is slated to begin recording their new album in three months. Three months! If Mathieu is gone for two of those months, there is no possible way to prepare for an entire album recording in thirty measly days. Adrien almost—almost—wishes that the famous Mathieu is indeed dead. It would make his job a whole lot easier and generate an enormous amount of free publicity for the label.

The thing is, Adrien Henri likes Mathieu. They aren't enemies, although they do clash heads often. They both have plenty of drive and ambition. Adrien's drive never drained, and his dedication is what landed him as a top dog in this industry and business, even without a major résumé of secondary industry. He made connections, bought the nicest clothes he could, worked odd jobs in popular venues, bartended, and networked until he finally landed a desk job.

From there, he proved himself to be the best, and he was noticed. People didn't want to mess with Adrien Henri, and eventually people in the music business wanted to be Adrien. He was a success story in the making, and he will be damned if Mathieu Deneuve takes even the slightest bit of that success away. It will not happen, it cannot happen if Adrien has anything to do with the future of Les Slinks.

Unfortunately for Mathieu, Adrien has everything to do with Les Slinks, and he has devised a plan. He hurriedly sits back in his chair. With one hand, he starts typing an e-mail, with the other hand he dials a number.

An emergency Les Slinks band meeting will be in session in less than twenty-four hours.

Sure, he has other bands on his label. There are two others. First, there is Christiane Blanche, a beautiful young woman with long blond hair and a giant bust. She, unfortunately, is proving to be a one-hit wonder. Then there is a band called the Artists—five boys barely out of high school—who has potential, but they are nowhere near the caliber of Les Slinks yet. Les Slinks and Mathieu have spark; they ignite the crowd. The crowds are loyal, and loyal crowds mean paychecks in the bank.

The next day at the meeting, Adrien gets started right on time. There isn't a minute to waste.

"All right, guys," Adrien starts. "Where could he be? I'm guessing one of you has talked to him. Time to confess!"

Marcel says, "Dude, we aren't on trial. We are here. We didn't do anything."

Pointing at Guillaume, Adrien says with an accusatory tone, "This one did. He let Mathieu get away. Why didn't you chase him?"

Guillaume chimes in, "You know the guy! He's crazy, insane. If Mathieu wants to be left alone, he will be left alone. He'll come back, and he'll have new lyrics. That's just Mathieu, and you know that."

"So what you are telling me is that no one in this room has any clue at all where this guy is? No one?" Adrien says, feeling exasperated and letting it show.

The band members are shaking their heads no and shrugging their shoulders. Adrien paces at the front of the room.

Marcel has an inkling suspicion of where Mathieu is hiding out. However, he has zero intentions of saying anything, let alone getting involved. Marcel is good friends with the entire Deneuve family and has Madeleine's direct e-mail. Not that he's used this lead yet, but he's only a message away, or so he thinks anyway.

Adrien continues on, arms flailing around as he speaks. "Since no one knows where he is or when he's coming back, we have no other option than to replace him."

"Replace him?" Oliver cries. "What are you talking about?"

"Dude, you can't replace the lead singer of our band," Marcel says.

"Yeah, man, the crowds come to see Mathieu, not an imposter," Oliver adds.

"I have a signed agreement, including Mathieu's signature, right here." He grabs a document and points to Mathieu's curvy, illegible signature on the contract. "I have the rights to replace him, if it will impact the band's success. Not being reachable is hurting your success."

"Can't we give him a week?" Guillaume asks.

"No," Adrien says firmly. "Recording starts in three months, and that is the end of it. You signed with me to take care of the business side of your band. This is business."

The band looks at each other with resignation, all of their expressions indicating a well-what-else-can-we-do attitude.

Marcel pipes up, "What if Mathieu comes back? In two months? Is he our main man again?"

"I can't give you that answer. The lead singer needs to be dependable," Adrien retorts.

"This is really unfair," Olivier says.

"No, what's unfair is Mathieu leaving all of you stranded, putting you in a bad position," Adrien says. "How humiliating is it to do those interviews for the TV and magazines and have your singer missing?"

"Do you know how long it will take to find someone?" Marcel says. "Forever!"

"I promise you that we will have new lead singer in six weeks or less," Adrien says, gaining momentum in his enthusiasm. His hand gestures become wilder as he continues. "I'm getting ready to announce the news that we are looking for the new face of Les Slinks, I'm going to set up auditions, and this will be the biggest news in musical history not only in France, but all over the world. This will generate media attention, it will generate new interest, new fans, and all of the current Les Slinks fans will want to see the new lead singer, and we are going to become the biggest, most successful band to ever come out of France. Ticket sales are going to soar!"

Marcel, who unfortunately is sitting right in front of Adrien in the meeting room, wipes away a drop of spit that hit him in the face as Adrien rambled on in his speech.

Olivier and Guillaume exchange worried looks. No one in this room besides Adrien is feeling hopeful about the looming changes, and they don't know what to say or what to do. Aside from being part of the band, Mathieu is a friend to these guys. You don't just give up on a friend.

Guillaume breaks the silence. "Guys, he has a point. Mathieu bailed. Why should we have to take a hit because of his Houdini act? I don't want to screw him over, but, man, do we have a choice?"

Adrien gives a smirk of satisfaction. "I'm glad you see it my way. Remember, it's nothing personal against Mathieu. This is a business, not a fraternity."

Marcel puts his hands on his face.

Not wanting to take any steps backward, Adrien continues persuading the band. "Look, it's this simple, guys. The greatest bands are assembled by a good business man"—he stops to clear his throat—"with a good eye. We just need a good front man. He needs charisma, stage presence, and a face that all the girls want to kiss."

"What about Marcel?" Guillaume suggests. "He's a great backup singer. He can move to the front, and we'll get a new backup."

"I like that idea," Olivier says.

Marcel looks up. "I like that more than finding a new singer."

"Marcel, you're great. But we need the wildness of Mathieu." Adrien quickly shuts that conversation down.

"Oh," Marcel says, looking disappointed, while the other guys look defeated.

"Six weeks, tops. Give it a chance. You are going to love the next chapter of Les Slinks. I've got a good feeling about all of this!" Adrien exclaims, imagining his dream house in the south.

CHAPTER NINE

*B*ack in Madeleine's apartment, Mathieu unscrews the lid to his whiskey bottle and takes a whiff of the liquor. He puts it back down and screws the top back on. Today, for the first time in months, probably even years, Mathieu resists the urge to take a swig from the clear glass bottle.

He puts the bottle back on the counter and steps out onto the porch, enjoying the freeness of the fresh air. He has no idea what to do.

I could watch more TV, he thinks, *or I could read a book.* He lets his mind drift to thoughts of the band. He has avoided looking at social media and the news because he honestly just doesn't care. However, his thoughts lure him to his bandmates, his friends.

He strikes up a slow tune on his air guitar and sits down on the petite white wicker sofa on the balcony. As he strums on his nonexistent instrument, he thinks about the guys. Are they mad? Surprised? Is Adrien giving them a hard time? Are they looking for him? Writing music in his absence? What would they think about Violette?

Violette!

He stops playing the air guitar and sits up straight. His heart flutters just at the mere thought of her name. *Violette Deschamps.* He lets his mind linger on those two words.

He leans back into the couch and lets out a sigh, but not an exasperated sigh. It's a calmer sigh, one that feels warm and relaxing as he releases it from his body.

He replays the events of their meeting in his mind, wondering what she thinks about him, and instantly regrets his obnoxious behavior.

"What is wrong with me?" he says aloud, thinking that the next time he sees her, he'll put on his charms, be on his best behavior.

Why do I care what she thinks? Mathieu wonders as he imagines the curve of her back that he couldn't help but study as she left the bistro the other day.

South of Paris, in her own flat, Violette lies awake in her bed, wishing she could fall asleep. She has tried counting to one hundred and counting backward from one hundred, but despite her best efforts, her mind keeps wandering. She rolls over on her side and bunches the warm covers up around her face, thinking how nice it would be to be a bear and just hibernate for an entire season.

She tries counting to one hundred again, but when she gets to twenty-three, Luc Deneuve's strikingly handsome face pops into her mind. She quickly tries to block the vivid image of him sitting at the bistro out of her mind by jumping to twenty-four, but the mental image leaves an echo.

Stop it, Violette. The guy is trouble, she tells herself, willing her mind to skip to the next scene in her attempt to fall asleep.

Giving up on the whole counting game, Violette turns to her other side. She has always been a side sleeper or a stomach sleeper, but never, ever does she sleep on her back. Since she can't get Luc off her brain, she tries the next best thing. She thinks of really awful, disgusting, unpleasant images to block him out.

She thinks of scary movies with their *dun-a, dun-a, dun-a* music leading up to *boo!*

moments, but Luc is there instead of the guy with the black mask and butcher cleaver.

"Well, this is just great," she whispers. *Go away, Luc. Get out of my mind.*

Finally, she just gives up and allows herself to think about him freely, not willing thoughts away or trying to suppress them. She lets her mind just be. As she replays the events of their meeting, she can't help but question who this guy really is and why he seems to be shrouded in secrecy. For a moment, her vivid imagination makes her question if he is an imposter, not Luc Deneuve, but some crazed maniac on the loose. She laughs at the thought. He seems harmless, just moody, and more importantly, she senses sadness in him.

Perhaps she recognizes his sadness because she knows what it looks like, what it feels like.

As she lies there in the dark, all is silent except for the ticking of the clock as the seconds go by—*tick, tick, tick* in an even pattern. Violette tries to remember the last time she had a boyfriend, let alone a date.

"Oh, good God," she says. It's been longer than she thought as she tallies up the math.

When she returned home from dropping out of school, she left Eduard behind. She thought that she would marry this guy. They had fun together, they loved each other well, and they tried doing long-distance dating, but with the demands of university for Eduard and the demands of caretaking of her mom and finding a job, the pair just drifted apart. One day they loved each other, and several months later, the love evaporated, slowly, like the morning dew.

Violette's heart aches at the very thought of their relationship. They haven't talked since Eduard came to break up with her in person. He was a kind and decent man, even in his wild days of college. He could have broken up with her over the phone, but no, he made the trek to see her, to kiss her good-bye one more time. They made promises to stay in touch.

Eduard told her, "Violette, I want you to stay in my life, as friends. I'd rather have you as a friend than not in my life at all."

While she wished desperately that it were the truth, once he hailed a cab and stepped in, she knew they would never speak to or see each other again.

So far, she has been correct in that prediction.

Eduard is as close to real love as she had ever come. In her eyes, it was real love, and she wonders if she'll ever have a taste of that sweet emotion once again.

After Eduard, Violette did go on some dates. She can count them on one hand or less.

She pulls her hand out from underneath the covers and counts on her fingers how long it has been since she has gone on a date, just to double-check. Starting with her thumb, one year, pointer finger, two years, and then she sits up straight in her bed.

Has it really been over two years since she has gone on a date? A real date? How? This thought befuddles her, haunts her, and instills a sense of fear and dread. For a moment, she is overcome with a typhoon wave of sadness.

It's not that she doesn't want a boyfriend, a fun date out. It's simply that she refuses to settle. None of the dates she went on compared with her Eduard, so she hadn't wasted her time with third or fourth dates. Instead, Violette accepts her adulthood is equivalent to that of an old maid. She has grown comfortable in the silence of coming home to an empty flat. No one cooks her dinner. No one cares for her when she is sick. The mere thought makes her empty, the fact that no one will care for her when she is old and gray.

Is she too picky?

Nope, she quickly tosses that theory out. One of the dates, was with a guy name Gerard.

Gerard was forty-five minutes late to pick her up, which was bad enough for someone as punctual as Violette, but it gets worse, much worse. They had to stop by his mother's house to pick up money for the date. This guy was in his thirties! How mortifying this was for Violette. She knew right then and there it was over before it started, but she couldn't escape this night of horror. He was nice enough, but no, just no.

Oh, how she would have loved to have said her I *do* to Eduard in a stunning white wedding dress in an intimate setting surrounded by only their closest friends and family. Oh, how she would have loved to have seen two pink lines show up on a pregnancy test and gleefully share the news in a playful way.

Instead, Violette thinks she really should get a cat.

And for a moment, just for fun, she has a preposterous idea. What would it be like to kiss Luc Deneuve for the first time? To move into one of the homes that she will be showing? What would it be like to snuggle with him on the couch after an ordinary, mundane day?

She thinks it sounds wonderful.

Maybe she can even help him decorate the place and turn it into his own personal palace.

Then her mind drifts just a little bit further. Since she is having an unusual case of insomnia and is feeling particularly whimsical, she plays around with how she would decorate his home, but not as Violette the decorator, as Violette Deneuve, homeowner and wife.

As she lies there, the hour of night unknown to her, she puts together color swatches of fabric and paint color and rugs. She places furniture in the bedroom, with accent colors, sheets, and draperies in a mix of grays and corals and whites. She imagines a farm-house-style table in the dining room, a casual funky mix that blends her style and his. She even allows herself the thought of decorating a nursery—for twins!

As these happy thoughts encroach the space between her current life and fantasy life, she feels the resemblance of a deep sleep settle over her. Her entire body relaxes, and as she slowly starts to dream, Luc is there, smiling and looking at her with loving eyes. Violette smiles in her dreams and falls deeper into a good night's sleep.

***

Knowing it's late but unsure of the exact time, Mathieu walks back inside the house and decides to go to sleep. A rare feeling, going to sleep clearheaded without a drop of liquor in his veins, he finds himself feeling an unexpected emotion... happiness. Tonight, he bypasses the couch to the bedroom. The room is small, but there is a real bed. After sleeping on tour buses for so long, a bed is a piece of luxury.

He pulls back the covers on the yellow eyelet quilt and climbs in. He lies in the silence of the room, just a ceiling fan buzzing softly, and he begins to hum the notes to a song he has yet to write.

CHAPTER TEN

*B*am! *Bam! Bam!*

Mathieu awakes, startled. He hears it again.

Bam! Bam! Bam!

"What the...?" he mutters.

Then he hears a voice.

"Mathieu! I know you're in there. Open up now." A voice yells from the other side of the door. "I'm not kidding. Mathieu. This isn't funny anymore."

Bam! Bam! Bam!

It's Marcel.

What should I do? Mathieu thinks, trying to come up with a plan. Perhaps more importantly, how does Marcel know where he is hiding?

"Come out this instant. Open this door. Adrien is furious."

Bam! Bam! Bam!

"I'm furious with you too, Mathieu, but I don't want you to get screwed over. Please, talk to me."

Mathieu ignores it. If he doesn't make a noise or turn on a light, he'll go away. He has to, eventually.

Bam! Bam! Bam!

Right, Mathieu thinks, *he will go away.*

Then silence.

Nothing.

Mathieu realizes he has been holding his breath in a frozen position. After a few moments of silence passes, Mathieu tiptoes ever so quietly to a window overlooking the front of the building. Marcel is back in his car, head hanging low.

Now his secret is out. Marcel knows where he is. And Mathieu has a feeling this won't be his last visit. He needs to get out, but where? He can't go back to his own home.

Wide-open spaces.

It's what he wants, and more importantly it's what he needs. His soul is aching and begging for a break from the claustrophobia of people and buildings, crammed together in the city like tiny sardines in a metal tin.

It's time to come up with Plan B.

He has already taken too many risks. Auguste, the cabbie, the grocery store.

He doesn't know exactly where he is going, but taxicabs are no longer a sufficient option, he decides. The next best thing is a personal driver and car service. He uses Madeleine's computer to locate a number. He dials the phone number and orders himself one town car and one personal driver. Of course, he emphasizes his need for privacy, although once again, he claims that his name is Luc Deneuve.

Once the driver and pickup time are arranged, Mathieu needs to come up with a place to go. His mind races like a Rolodex of business cards, each flashing images of his favorite luxury hotels, but none of them seem to resonate well with him.

"Think, Mathieu, think," he says. "Aha!" He has the perfect solution.

He sits back down at the computer and searches for bed and breakfasts.

This one looks good, he thinks, and fortunately, there is room at the inn.

There is just one last item to take care of before Mathieu flees the city limits of Paris. Calling Madeleine.

She picks up on the first ring.

"There is my big brother!" she says upon answering. They have a running joke that he is older since he was born precisely two minutes before her.

"Hey, sis." It feels good to talk to a familiar voice.

"Where'd you run off to? I was worried about you!" she says with genuine concern.

"Your place, actually."

"My place? Hmm, I'm going to have to remember to change the locks on my doors!" she says with laughter.

"Always the funny one. I just wanted to let you know that I crashed at your place, but that I'm heading out. I wanted someone to know where I was going. Please keep this secret. Only for emergencies do I want to be contacted."

"Mathieu, are you in trouble?"

There's a pause.

"Mathieu?" she says, "Are you there?"

"No trouble. I just... I just need a change of scenery for a bit."

"If you say so. Well, listen, I got to get back on set."

"Sounds good. Just write down this number and keep it close to you."

He rattles off the phone number for the inn.

"Talk soon, Mad!"

"Bye. *Bisous*."

Once they get off the phone, Mathieu is relieved and thankful for such a close relationship with his twin. He knows he can trust her with anything. It's part of the built-in twin code.

***

Meanwhile in Prague, Madeleine slips the piece of scrap paper with Mathieu's name and number scribbled on it into her pocket and hurries back to her spot behind the cameras. On her short walk back to the set, the small piece of paper flies out of Madeleine's pocket and floats into the air behind her.

***

Mathieu thanks his driver, steps out of the backseat of his rented town car, and looks around the grounds of his newest home, sweet home, the Little Rose Bed and Breakfast. He isn't quite sure what to make of the place, but the grounds are enchanting. Cobblestone pathways, an open field, rose bushes in every color, charming porches on the front and side of the house. It's unusual, Mathieu thinks, as this is so not his normal setting.

He opens the front door to the Little Rose, and no one is there. For a minute he thinks he has the wrong address. Did the driver get the address wrong? *How hard is it to follow directions?*

He turns to leave, but then a young man, probably not older than sixteen, appears on the stairway, his mouth hanging open, gawking.

"Er, I think I have the wrong address," Mathieu says.

"You aren't Mathieu Deneuve, are you?" the young man says.

"Who wants to know?" he asks in return.

The boy walks down the stairs and goes behind an antique desk that has a little sign that Mathieu didn't see before.

Welcome to the Little Rose Bed & Breakfast.

So he is in the right place.

"I'm a huge fan of yours. Can I shake your hand? Have your autograph?"

"Albert, that is no way to talk to our guest. You should be ashamed of yourself!" A woman comes barreling from the back of the house.

"Mr. Deneuve, welcome to our inn. Please excuse my son," she says, giving Albert a warning look. "I'm Elle Beland, proprietor of the Little Rose."

"Mom, this is Mathieu Deneuve of Les Slinks!"

"Albert, stop," his mother says with a tone of finality. "I do not care of he is the president of France! All of our guests are treated with the same hospitality. Now, take Mr. Deneuve's bag up to his room. And no questions. Give the man some peace!" She then turns her gaze back to Mathieu. "I'm terribly sorry, sir. Welcome again. I promise you, I will speak to my boy and make sure there are no disturbances. Breakfast is at eight. Let us know if you need anything."

"Thank you," Mathieu says bowing his head slightly to the plump women with wild red hair.

Albert reappears.

"Albert, please apologize to Mr. Deneuve and take him to his room."

"I'm sorry, sir," he says, looking mortified. No teen wants to be embarrassed by his mother, but being scolded in front of a rock star?

Remembering what it was like to be his age, Mathieu smiles at Albert, shakes his hand, and tells him his mom is just like his. Not entirely true, but a good deed for the day. He follows the teen up the stairs and down a small hallway on the left, and they stop at a wood door with the number three on it.

"Here is your room," Albert says before turning and leaving Mathieu to himself.

"Thanks, buddy," he says.

Albert beams.

Mathieu opens the door, and his eyes hurt at the sight. The décor is so hideous, but somehow the room looks put together. Mathieu hasn't seen anything quite like this before. Everywhere he looks there are knickknacks, and the room is crammed with furniture. The bedspread covering the four-poster bed must be at least sixty years old, covered with a homemade quilt donning roses of pink and red tones. A fresh vase of red roses, probably two dozen at least, fill a vase by the large bay window overlooking the stunning backyard.

He imagines sitting under the small gazebo with Violette. *Why do I keep thinking about her?* He decides to spend some time checking out the homes she recommended for him, but realizes he doesn't have a computer.

He goes back downstairs and asks Elle if she has a computer he can borrow.

"Let's see. We have this old thing," she says, pointing to a dated computer.

Albert comes to the rescue. "You can use my laptop if you'd wish. Mom didn't want me to have one, but I needed it for school."

"I would love to use it, just for the afternoon."

"Anytime! Just let me know. Hang on, I'll go grab it."

Albert brings the computer right out, and even though the inn's décor is far from his taste, Mathieu does appreciate the warm hospitality.

Once in his room, he sits at the bay window overlooking the yard and peruses the list of homes Violette sent. Some of them are spectacular, truly. One in particular grabs his eye. There is something that feels welcoming in the pictures.

As he looks through the site, he can't help but think of Violette and how different she is from the women who constantly surround him in his life. He is so used to the young and the wild. While Violette is still fairly young, she doesn't seem wild at all. Not boring, just not wild. He wonders if she has ever been drunk and how she remains so grounded, not self-involved, like himself, a flaw he recognizes.

From their one meeting, he thinks he knows Violette. Calm, sober... and so relatable. He hardly knows her, he reasons. But she has already impacted him, and he cannot wait to see these houses, and her.

Violette seems to be his muse, for every time he thinks about her, he feels like singing and humming a new tune. Lyrics and word snippets flash into his mind, and he feels himself beating along to a new drum.

What he needs is his guitar, an extended extremity of his body. He needs to feel the strum of the strings against his fingers, and he needs to let the sweet sounds fill his world. He has one back at his apartment, but the question is, how does he get it?

CHAPTER ELEVEN

The next morning, Mathieu is greeted by the most delicious smells coming from the downstairs kitchen. He puts on his signature distressed jeans and a clean T-shirt and runs his hands through his hair. His stomach grumbles.

"Wow," Mathieu says, when he sees the food spread on the table in the dining room. A prosciutto and cheese plate, a pile of pastries, and a fruit plate.

"All breads are made in house every morning," Elle says to him. "Now, let me grab you a plate. Eat! Eat!"

"Do you do this every morning? Even when no other guests are here?" Mathieu asks.

"Absolutely. My boy needs a good meal before school, and baking is my specialty. I sell to local bakeries."

"This looks incredible." Mathieu grabs an almond croissant in honor of his new friend, Violette.

Albert is already sitting at the table and munching on a slice of white cheese.

Elle takes his drink order and returns to the kitchen. When she is safely out of earshot, Mathieu turns to Albert.

"Can you do me a favor?" he asks the teen in a whisper.

"Sure," Albert says.

"I need you to get my guitar from my apartment. Can you please get it for me?"

"Um, yeah!"

"Okay, I'll pay you. Just make sure it's only you who goes. No friends. Keep this a secret between us. Got it?"

"Not a word," Albert says, looking thrilled with his secret mission. "I've always wanted to play an instrument."

"I'll let you while I'm here. I'll teach you a few basics."

"No way. That's awesome!" Albert says right as his mom comes back in with a fresh latte for her guest.

"What's awesome?" Elle asks.

"Nothing, just guy talk," Mathieu says, winking at his new friend.

The three of them eat their breakfast, and Mathieu wonders if the inn is doing okay financially. He is the only guest, which is fine by him. He also wonders about a Mr. Beland. There has been no mention of Albert's father or Elle's husband. Either way, he likes the warm, comfortable atmosphere of their eclectic home. It reminds him of his childhood house back in Montmartre.

"So, Mathieu, how long are you staying here?" Albert asks.

"Don't pry, dear," Elle says, giving Albert a warning look.

Mathieu laughs, as he has gotten that look hundreds of times.

"Oh, it's fine, I promise. I'm house hunting at the moment, and as soon as I find a place, I'll be out of your hair. I'm thinking a month, tops?"

"A month?" The mother and son duo exchange pleased glances.

"If that's all right, of course," Mathieu adds.

"Of course, dear," Elle says, "Our home is your home."

Mathieu realizes that his mood hasn't been as temperamental as usual, and he is enjoying the change of pace immensely, so much so that he offers to help out around the house. The words are a shock to him as they spill out.

"Dear, you are a guest. Nonsense!" Elle says.

"Well, the offer stands," Mathieu says as he grabs another slice of meat off the plate in the center of the table.

Once the breakfast dishes are cleared, Albert and Mathieu get a moment alone.

"Are you free to get my guitar after your lessons today?"

"Just tell me what to do!" Albert says, giving a little salute.

"Okay, here is my address. Do not lose it. Do not give it to anyone. Do not copy it." He hands a slip of paper to Albert. "And here is a key. Make sure no one sees you go in. It's of grave importance that you keep this mission top secret. No bragging to your friends or anyone. Got it?"

"You sound like my mother, but I won't breathe a word of this to a soul. I promise.

Besides, I really want to learn how to play the guitar. Your secret is safe with me."

Albert heads out the door for the day, and Mathieu stands in the doorway, hoping he hasn't just made a giant mistake.

***

Mathieu is at a loss for what to do here at the Little Rose Bed and Breakfast. The pace is so much slower that he can almost feel each minute tick by. He chooses a book from the bookshelf and reads outside, soaking in some sunshine and these gorgeous grounds. And after lunch, he decides it is time to call Violette. He is ready to schedule a tour of some of the properties.

As he goes to dial her office number on the business card she gave him, he feels nervous.

"Thank you for calling Domaines D'Elegance. This is Violette Deschamps."

"Violette, hi. It's Mat—er, Luc Deneuve. How are you?"

"Luc? It's good to hear from you. What can I do for you today?"

He really wants to ask her to dinner, but sticks to business. "Well, I spent some time going through the listings you gave me, and I want to go look at some. I have the list ready, and it's quite a few actually."

Mathieu has added a few extra properties to the list just to try to spend some more time with the woman. *It'll be fun*, he thinks.

"I'm interested in seeing these potential homes as soon as possible. I'd love for you to clear your entire schedule for the next couple of weeks because you are going to be seeing a whole lot of me. I'm ready to buy, and I'm ready to buy right now."

"You certainly sound more enthusiastic," Violette says with a chuckle. "I can spend about half the day with you tomorrow showing you a few places. I'll go around and make the arrangements for about four houses. Will that suit you?"

"Yes, and I can pick you up. I'll hire a car to take us around. It will make it easier."

"I have a car," Violette says. "I'll drive. Do you want me to pick you up?"

"Oh." Mathieu does not want Violette to know he's staying in a bed and breakfast. "No, that's okay. I'll be in your area. I'll stop by the office around noon. How's that?"

"Great. See you tomorrow, Luc."

"Good-bye, Violette." He hangs up, wishing there was more of a reason to keep her on the line.

***

Later that evening, Mathieu is in his room when he hears the door open and Albert's voice.

He walks to the top of the stairs and breathes a sigh of relief to see his black guitar case. His case is covered with stickers, mainly bumper stickers, from all of the places he has toured, a keepsake of his life on stage.

"Hey, Albert," Mathieu says.

"I got your guitar, but I think there's something that I need to tell you," Albert says with such a grave tone.

Oh God, Mathieu thinks, *the word is out.* Albert just kind of looks at him, and Mathieu begins to grow agitated.

"Well, what is it then?" It comes out a little snappier than he intended.

"Not around Mom, please?" Albert replies, which makes Mathieu even more nervous.

"Let me just put this in my room, and we'll go for a short stroll." Mathieu grabs the case and goes to set it down. When he comes back out, the pair walk to the back door. Mathieu again asks what is going on.

"Well, I got to your apartment, and there was a man in there."

This catches Mathieu completely off guard. "What do you mean? There was a man in there?" Mathieu feels alarmed, and adrenaline is pumping through body. "Who was it? What did he look like?"

"He was tall, skinny. Brown hair, kind of pale. He said his name was Marcel."

"What was he doing? What did he say? What did you say?"

Albert looks utterly bewildered with all the questions.

Mathieu continues the questioning, his rage becoming more evident.

"Tell me what happened," Mathieu says in a low roar that terrifies Albert.

"I walked in, and there he was," Albert starts.

"And then?"

"He jumped! I think I scared him. He asked who I was and what I was doing there."

"For goodness sake, Albert, what did you say?"

"I didn't say anything, actually. He looked angry, very angry, kind of like how you look right now."

Mathieu feels ashamed at the comment. Albert's just trying to help. "I'm sorry I snapped at you. It's not you. It's the stress."

"It's okay," Albert says, relaxing.

"Then what happened?"

"Okay, the guy, Marcel, when he realizes I'm not going to answer his questions, he says, 'Oh, never mind,' and grabs a pen and a piece of paper. He scribbles this note and says, 'Give this to Mathieu. I know you know where he is.'"

"And that's it?"

"Well, not exactly," Albert says.

"What do you mean, not exactly? I need to know exactly what happened."

"After he hands me the note, he asks me who I am, my name, how I know you."

"And..." Mathieu says, indicating for Albert to finish the rest of the story already.

"I told him that I was your cousin and that my name is Andre. He didn't believe me, he said he knows your family well and there has never been a cousin Andre in the family. That's it. He stormed out the door, I grabbed your guitar case, and here we are."

As he says that, Elle comes out of the house and waves to them.

"Albert, you aren't bothering our guest, are you?"

Mathieu answers for him. "Not at all. We were just having a chat and I was planning to show Albert how to play a few chords on my guitar later."

Elle looks pleased. "Well, go ahead. I won't interrupt."

She turns to go back inside, stops, and whips her head back to them.

"Mathieu, doll, would you like to have dinner with us? I don't normally ask guests, but it's so quiet this week, and, well, it's nice having you around."

Mathieu takes her up on the invitation and with a satisfied nod, Elle retreats to get started on their supper.

"Are you really going to teach me how to play guitar right now?" Albert asks.

"Yes, indeed, bud." He slips the note from Marcel in his pocket.

In his room, Mathieu unclips the hinges on his beloved guitar case.

Albert is terrible. In fact, Mathieu has never heard someone play an instrument in a way that makes it sound like someone is torturing puppies.

"I'm dreadful at this, aren't I?"

"You aren't great," Mathieu says with a playful laugh. "I was really bad when I started, as well. My siblings would all groan and beg me not to play. I never gave up though. C'mon, let's keep going."

A little while later, Elle comes out, wiping her hands on a dishcloth. "Dinner is served!" she announces.

Mathieu thinks it smells wonderful, more wonderful than their breakfast feast.

At the table, Mathieu is greeted with a pot roast on a bed of potatoes and carrots alongside fresh green beans sprinkled with lemon zest.

"Come, sit, sit." Elle ushers them around the table.

"Don't you ever grow tired of cooking for all your guests?" Mathieu asks with genuine curiosity.

"Oh, my dear boy," Elle says, looking sad and worn out.

She starts to continue, but Albert pipes up, "Business has been slow. It's why Mom has been selling her food at the bakeries and farmers markets."

"Albert Beland, we do not talk like that around our guests!" she says with a sheepish, embarrassed look, her cheeks reddening.

"It's true," Albert says, ignoring his mom. "She works all the time, ever since Dad died."

"Albert, that's enough!" Elle says. "Not in front of our guest."

Mathieu isn't sure what to say or do.

"I'm sorry to hear about your father's passing, and your husband's."

"Well, now, this talk is much too serious for the dinner table," she says, giving Albert another one of her mom looks, begging him not to say another word.

Mathieu changes the topic to Albert's guitar lesson, but the lighthearted conversation is a façade. In the back of his mind, Mathieu is intrigued by the story of Mr. Beland. To think that Albert lost his father so young is heartbreaking.

After dinner, Elle announces that Albert has homework to do, and Mathieu retreats to his bedroom in the ramshackle inn to finally pull out the note with Marcel's handwriting.

The note says: *Mathieu, this is urgent. Call me ASAP! Please, for your own sake.*

Mathieu crumples up the note and throws it in the small trash can sitting by the desk in his suite. He pulls out his guitar and quietly strums a new riff for a possible song that he keeps hearing in his head.

CHAPTER TWELVE

"*A*fter you," Mathieu says to Violette, opening the door of her own car for her.

"Thanks!" she says politely before gracefully stepping into the driver's seat

Mathieu can't help but notice that Violette looks like a different person now that she isn't wearing that horrid, ill-fitting suit. Since he is in a playful mood, he calls her out on it.

"You look so much more comfortable today than you did at the bistro," Mathieu says with a boyish grin as they buckle up, scoping Violette out for her response.

"This is much more my usual style." She is in a simple cotton dress, a cardigan over her shoulders, and a pair of flats.

"Why were you all dressed up then? In that awful suit?"

Violette turns one hundred different shades of red, the colors of beets and strawberries and Santa Claus hats all in one.

"I'm kidding. Bad joke?" he says, chuckling at her reaction.

"Can I tell you a secret?" she asks.

"Oh, a secret, I like it!"

"My boss made me change clothes."

"You're kidding. For me?"

"I tell no lies," she says.

At the mention of the word *lie*, a guilty shiver climbs up his back, and he wishes he could tell her that he is really Mathieu, not Luc.

"That's insane," he says. "Why?"

"Only the best for Madeleine's brother!"

Mathieu rolls his eyes, and his expression turns serious.

"Just to be clear, I did ask for discretion."

"Oh, I know. Please don't worry. Jean-Philippe is in the know with all the clients and realtors. It's part of his job."

Violette regrets saying anything at all, and Mathieu can tell it has made her uncomfortable.

Violette recovers by adding, "Besides, I treat all my clients the same. I don't care if you are Prince William or a famous actor. My job is help you find your best home."

The irony, Mathieu thinks.

The first of the four homes they are scheduled to tour is an opulent estate. Mathieu isn't sure what he wants, so he has decided to have Violette show all of them. If he doesn't find anything, Violette hopes to gain a better idea of what he wants after today.

"This place is nice," he says when they walk up to the front door. It looks like something out of a magazine, and even Violette gawks at the grandiose look of the Tudor-style home.

Inside, the home has every feature imaginable. No detail has been left untouched in this older, completely renovated minipalace. This is a home fit for the Queen of England herself.

As they weave in and out of the many rooms, Violette points out features such as the coffered ceilings, hand-carved cabinets, and custom granite.

"What do you think of this place?" he asks Violette.

"It doesn't matter what I think," she says. "It's all about what feels like a home to you. Do you like it?"

"I'd be crazy not to," he says.

"This home is move-in ready. You wouldn't have to complete any renovations, which seemed to be an issue for you last time."

"Well, this place can stay on the possible list."

Progress, Violette thinks. The house feels cold—beautiful, yes—but it needs warm tones. Violette's imagination veers off, and she thinks the house feels like tragedy. Each house has a story to share, and in every house Violette shows, she wonders about the stories that the home holds. She often imagines the characters who make of the cast of legacies that are inter-linked and woven within the walls.

Of course, none of this would ever be uttered to a client, especially not one like Luc.

As they walk out the door and back to their chariot, Mathieu and Violette both go to open the front door at the same time and their hands graze. Mathieu's hands lie on top of Violette's, and he lets it linger. The softness, her delicacy, sends a zing of shivers down his spine, and he wishes that he could hold on.

Violette likes the feel of his masculine hands. She can feel the callous roughness of his fingers. It's been so long since she felt human connection, and she wishes it were something more than just a graze of a door being opened. The touch makes her dizzy, and she can't bring herself to make eye contact with Luc. So she ignores it, pretends this tiny incident never happened.

Mathieu is disheartened by Violette's reaction, or lack of reaction. *Nothing?* he thinks. Women can't resist him! They faint in his presence!

This has never happened. Well, not since his nerdy days before he was a musician. Back then he was turned down more times than he would ever like to admit. Clearly, Violette felt absolutely nothing. He feels ridiculous that such a little gesture could mean anything.

Violette diverts the awkwardness of the situation by asking him, "So, Luc, is there anything you don't like about this property?"

"Hmm." He thinks. "It needs more character. It feels huge and giant and empty."

The next house that they visit is much different than the first. It's a cottage, much warmer and smaller than the previous.

"This place is charming," Mathieu says at first glance.

A *good start*, Violette thinks. And it is charming. An older home, the cottage is made of a light-brown stone with blue-sky shutters framing the windows.

As they are walking through this house, Mathieu decides to have a little fun.

"So, is this the kind of house your husband would like?"

"*What?*" she says with great surprise, totally caught off guard by the absurdity and personal nature of his question.

"I said, is this the kind of house your husband would like?"

"No, I heard you. I don't have a husband."

"Boyfriend? Fiancé?"

"I think you should be picturing yourself here with your own girlfriend or wife and kids."

They walk into the kitchen, which is small and dated but has a certain homey charm that makes Violette swoon. She would love a place like this. Mathieu leans up against the counters.

"Why not?" he prods.

"That's none of your business," she says with a mildly flirtatious tone that she doesn't mean to have.

"Have you ever been married?" he says, pushing his luck with a flirtatious tone right back at her.

"Luc, look at the kitchen."

"A kitchen is a kitchen."

Violette rolls her eyes.

"No, I'm serious! So, c'mon, just tell me. Have you ever been married?"

They walk through the small powder room on the downstairs level. They are both crammed in the tiny room, and Violette thinks he has gotten closer on purpose. She ponders the magnitude of his question, and the true answer makes her sad. Alone and no prospects.

I'm just imagining things, Violette tells herself. *Luc Deneuve is not flirting with me.* Wishful thinking!

"Fine, I'll tell you. No boyfriend, no fiancé, and no husband. Never been married. Happy?" Then, to mix things up, she adds, "But I do have a potential date."

A date? This certainly intrigues Mathieu, so of course, he prods into the matter further. Realtor investigation, he calls it. "What's he like, this guy?"

Truth be told, she has no idea. She's thinking of Jean-Philippe's nephew, who she has never met. It's a better story than being totally alone, at least in Violette's opinion.

And for a moment, he actually feels jealous. He wants to take her on a date, a real date.

"My turn. Girlfriend?"

"Nope. Just me and my music and my soon-to-be-new house!"

"Is this the one?" she asks him as she locks the door behind them.

"I like it, more family-friendly feeling, but I'm not sure it throws off good bachelor vibes. It needs to be fancier."

What does this guy want? Violette thinks. No wonder he's single! Too stately, not fancy enough, maybe house number three will resonate with her picky client.

The third house is traditional. It's all brick and is the type of house that passersby on the street stop to admire.

This house, Violette feels, is a blend of previous houses, but of course, it's all about what Luc wants.

Mathieu is wowed by the grand staircase upon entering the home, and Violette starts to relax. He seems to be in such a better mood than he was before, and Violette thinks maybe she wrote him off as depressed and morose too soon.

The bedrooms in this place are large and full of natural light. It's a bright home that could use some new paint. Violette thinks choosing the colors would be like creating a master-piece. When decorating, Violette doesn't choose one style, like minimalist, chic, or art deco. Instead, she picks up on a vibe from the original structure and creates a palette that enhances the room like makeup enhances the face of a woman. The original beauty shines through, but the design adds a warm, inviting feel.

As Violette points out the positives and negatives about the house, she notices that Luc keeps looking at her, intensely, with his sparkling blue eyes. Whenever their eyes lock, she feels as if she is in a movie, the star of a love story. She always quickly breaks the gaze, yet he persists.

Violette, she tells herself, *stop it! None of this means anything.*

Mathieu on the other hand, thoroughly enjoys all of this flirting. He loves that he is finally having an effect on this adorable woman. She's trying to play hard to get, and he is up for a good game of chase.

"What about kids?" he asks.

"What about them?"

"Do you have any?"

Oops, this might have been too far, he tells himself when he sees her face turn red instantly.

"No!" Who does he think she is?

"Relax, it was a joke. I'm just kidding!"

She ignores him.

After this tour, she once again asks him the famous real estate question, "What did you think of this place?"

"It's good. I like it. I like the other two as well. I'm not sure any of them are 'it' though. I'm looking for a feeling, something soulful. I can't explain it, but I will know it when I see it. Does that make sense?"

Actually it does to Violette. She is the same way, but that means this hunt is going to take forever. She makes a mental note of the word *soulful* and thinks that house number four won't have the soulful vibe he is looking for. It's modern, funky, and completely unlike the other three. Violette feels as though she is showing houses to four completely different clients, as these houses have very little in common. Unfortunately, she still can't figure out what his dream house is.

House number four is a new construction house with an urban feel. It's very minimalistic in style with clean lines and sleek extras, like the black sink in the kitchen.

"This is what I think of as a bachelor pad," she says.

"I just feel as though I need to throw a party here, which is not what I'm looking for."

"You are picky," Violette states matter-of-factly.

"That, I am," he says with a smile.

They step out onto the amazing back porch that has a stone fire pit where the flames light up in a straight line surrounded by rocks.

"Violette, I must ask you, what do you do outside of work?"

Once again, his question catches her off guard.

She pauses for a minute, and he watches her as she is deep in thought.

"I spend a lot of time taking care of my mom. And I work."

"I bet she appreciates it."

"She does." The words slip out, and she knows she can't stop there. "She is my family. She is all I have, so we are really close. "

Thinking of his own loud, crazy, and big family, he can't imagine growing up without his brothers and sisters. There was always someone to pick on, always someone to play with, and always someone to fight with.

"What do you do for fun? For you?" he says, cocking his head, with a gentle tone.

"I love interior design."

She tells him about some of her projects around her own flat, and he seems genuinely interested.

"I'm also an avid reader. I love a good mystery."

Mathieu pictures her curled up on a couch and wishes he could cuddle up right beside her.

In a moment of spontaneity, Mathieu interrupts Violette.

"Would you have dinner with me? Tonight? It'll be fun, I promise."

Violette thinks about saying yes; she wants to say yes. She is flattered and feels shy all of the sudden.

"I can't."

"Oh?"

"I have to fill out some papers for Mom tonight."

"You are a mystery, Violette Deschamps," he says, winking at her. "Maybe I should write a mystery book about you, my new friend."

"How would it end?" she asks playfully.

"That's the mystery part," he responds mischievously.

On their way back to the office, Mathieu is disappointed. He's disappointed that he hasn't found his house and disappointed that Violette turned him down. He thinks to himself that she clearly isn't interested, and he makes up his mind to forget his infatuation. He wills himself to keep her off his mind. Game over.

CHAPTER THIRTEEN

*V*iolette didn't lie to Luc. She really does have to sign some papers as her mother's power of attorney this evening. The truth is, she would have loved to have dinner with him. If she is honest with herself, she would love to have dinner with anyone. She doesn't have a lot of friends, and she is lonely. Her short burst of time with her newest, incredibly attractive client has shown her that.

However, Luc seems so different. He's so... edgy and spontaneous. They wouldn't be a good fit in the long run. After all, Violette has her responsibilities with her mother, and he might get bored once he realizes how boring her life really is. The last thing she needs is to be heartbroken again.

After their meeting, Violette is back at Domaines D'Elegance, sitting at her desk making a few notes from the home tours. She's mainly trying to connect the dots as to what this guy wants in a home. It's not that he is difficult, but rather just indecisive, which is exactly what she tells Jean-Philippe when he asks how the showings went.

"Violette, you know how important closing this deal will be, don't you?"

She doesn't appreciate his brisk tone.

"You know I do, but I'm not going to force someone to buy a house. It has to be the right house. My job is not being a pushy salesperson."

Jean-Philippe nods his head in agreement, surrendering to the fact she is right.

"You are one of the good ones," he says, wagging his finger at her. He walks out her door.

She finishes up her notes and is just about to leave for the evening when Jean-Philippe and another man appear at her door.

"Oh, Violette!" Jean-Philippe says, acting peculiar and surprised to see her.

It has been only fifteen minutes since they last spoke.

"My nephew, Etienne, is in town. He's new to Paris," he says this with a wink. "I'm introducing him to folks around the office and helping him navigate the City of Love!"

Gosh, how awkward can he be? Violette thinks. First he tries to set her up and now he ambushes her?

"Etienne, nice to meet you," Violette says politely, extending her hand for a shake.

"Lovely to meet you. I've heard so many good things about you. I hope we can grab coffee sometime?"

Violette knows she should probably say yes, just to be nice. She wills herself to say yes, but she cannot. She is not attracted to this man in the slightest bit. He looks just like Jean-Philippe, just a younger version, of course. Violette could never go on a date with someone who looked like her boss and father figure. It would be much too weird.

"Etienne, I have to tell you. My schedule is slammed, and I'm just not sure when I would have time."

Fortunately, Jean-Philippe takes a stance to support Violette. He knows her well enough to practically read her mind.

"Violette is working with a huge client right now, I should have known better than to suggest coffee. Anyway, we are out of here for an early dinner."

"Nice meeting you," Violette calls out while secretly cursing Jean-Philippe.

"And you don't work too late, young lady."

Violette hangs out in her office for another ten minutes to make sure they are gone. When she thinks the path is clear, she locks up and makes the short drive over to the hospice, wishing that Etienne had been different.

Am I just too picky? she asks herself, a question she seems to be asking a lot lately.

The thought is quickly banished when she walks into the hospice and turns her attention solely to her mother.

Nadine isn't there tonight, so a different, new nurse lets her in.

When she gets to her mother's room, she finds herself particularly chatty. She sits in the chair by her mother's bed and talks to her mother as if she can understand her. She talks to her mom as if she can respond.

"I have a new client," she starts. "His name is Luc, and he is incredibly gorgeous and strange and moody and wonderful."

Violette surprises herself by how much she is talking about Luc. She tells her mother all about her day and the showings. She describes the homes, and she talks as if she is talking to a girlfriend, overanalyzing the details of their hand graze. She questions whether or not he was flirting or whether it was all in her imagination.

As she talks, her mom smiles in her sleep. This sends a chill of calmness through Violette's body, as if she were driving through a field of wild lavender. Her conversation morphs into tales of wishful thinking.

She tells her mom that she wishes she could be there when she walks down the aisle, that she could help her put on a wedding dress, that she could meet her future fiancé.

She tells her mom that she wishes that she would be able to hold her first grandchild. If it's a girl, Violette promises to use Lydia as a first or middle name.

The questions that Luc asked her earlier about love and kids seem to haunt her. The questions have ignited a sense of longing and desire deep within Violette. Would she be crazy to try online dating? It's worked for thousands of couples according to the websites. Maybe she could have a fairy-tale ending after all.

She even allows herself to picture a fairy-tale ending with Luc, but quickly brushes that thought aside, like a crumb is brushed off a coat. The mere thought of a happily-ever-after with Luc makes her body tingle and both her stomach and heart flutter.

Does he really like her that way? They're so different.

She starts fixing her mom's hair, and as she gets the curlers and hairspray, she wonders what would have happened if Luc had never come into her life as a client. Would they pass each other on the street? Would their paths never have crossed? Would it even have mattered?

As Violette wraps a thin strand of her mother's hair in a curler, she feels an urgency to talk about her childhood.

Violette was a blessing to her parents later in their lives. They both wanted a big family, kids playing in the backyard, chaos around the dinner table, but they could never conceive. Violette was a surprise, but she knows she was a welcome surprise. Violette understands that her mother and father never took her for granted because of this.

Growing up, Violette sometimes resented that there was such a large generation gap between her parents and herself. Sometimes they just didn't get the latest trends or they seemed so old-fashioned compared to her friends' parents. Now, Violette is just appreciative that she had the opportunity to call them hers.

Violette brings up some of her childhood memories and laughs about them as she recalls them to her mother.

The time she went digging in the creek behind their house and brought a black snake into their kitchen. Her mother screamed so loud that it startled Violette and she dropped the snake. They didn't find that snake again for three days.

The time she had her first date and her father made the guy sit on the couch for a little guy talk. Violette was mortified.

The time they toured the beautiful Brittany region of northern France, eating and tasting their way through all the cafés and wineries that abound.

For the longest time, Violette has been frustrated about her mom being sick and leaving her. *Why?* she would question. *Why? Why my mother?*

Tonight, as she grabs another curler and tangles it around the thin, white strands, Violette says to her mother, "I'm so sorry you are sick, Mom. I'm not mad at you in the slightest. I will be fine. I hope you know how proud of you I am, for everything you are and for everything you have done for me."

Her mother smiles softly in her sleep, and Violette hopes she understands what she is saying.

"Life never turns out like we expect, does it? But, Mom, I'm all right. I have a good job that I enjoy and a cozy flat that is all mine. I have a future, and I always want you and Daddy to be proud of who I have become."

She gazes at her mother and squeezes her hand. Lydia looks cold, so Violette grabs a brightly colored blanket from the closet and layers it on top of the thin, white sheets.

"Who knows? Maybe one day I'll be able to be a wife and a mom and a realtor all at the same time. If not, I will still make my own dreams come true."

Violette envisions the house of her dreams and tells her mom about it.

"One day, I want to own my home, not a flat, but a detached home. It's going to be cozy and warm, a small cottage, nothing too big. I'm going to decorate with a modern farmhouse chic style. My home will have a garden, just like the one you and Dad had in our backyard. I'll grow herbs and vegetables. Of course, I'll have a rosemary bush," Violette says, reminiscing about their rosemary bush that lived through snow and heat and had the endurance of a marathon runner.

"*This thing will never die!*" she says, imitating her father in his joking voice.

But eventually, it did die, as all things must.

Violette knows it's inevitable, but she can't bring herself to think about what will happen when her mother passes away. It's unbearable.

"Also, with my future home, I'm going to get a dog. I'd love to get a puppy, maybe a golden-doodle, a cross between a golden retriever and a poodle, but I'd also love to rescue an older dog, one that needs a home and has no one else."

When Violette looks at the clock, she realizes that she has been visiting for much longer than normal, yet she can't bring herself to leave. Instead, she grabs her book and starts reading the next chapter aloud.

After three chapters, Violette starts dozing off. She finishes her nightly routine by humming along to a song on the radio. Finally, she kisses her mother's cheeks good-bye and slowly makes her way home.

***

Back at the Little Rose Bed and Breakfast, Mathieu has spent the evening mulling over potential house choices, thinking about Violette, and toying around with lyrics to a new song. He almost, almost considers calling Marcel back, but decides against it. In order for creativity to flourish, Mathieu reasons, he needs to have space for the creativity to grow.

As he gets ready to go sleep, once again without a drop of alcohol running through his veins, Mathieu falls into a restless sleep, his mind racing in a myriad of directions. The band, the house search, Violette, the lyrics that he can't perfect, Marcel's note—he can't seem to compartmentalize his thoughts.

Once he finally falls asleep, he dreams. He dreams of Violette's chocolate brown eyes and waking up next to her in their dream house.

CHAPTER FOURTEEN

Mathieu quickly pulls his pants over his legs and throws a graphic T-shirt on. He knows he needs to figure out what he's going to do. He only has a few weeks left before he plans to meet up with the band again. While he knows he can be moody and difficult, he always keeps his word. Les Slinks is his second family.

Violette is scheduled to show him a few more properties, and he can't wait to see her. Even though he promised and swore to himself that he would not try to flirt with this woman, and he begged himself to forget this infatuation, he simply cannot. This woman, this slightly unfashionable and incredibly charming woman, has a grasp on him. No matter what he does, he cannot seem to forget her. She drives him mad, she drives him wild... and she isn't even doing a thing. He can't explain it. Being around her simply makes him smile.

And he is determined to make her like him. As pompous as this sounds, he is irritated that she doesn't seem to like him as much as he likes her.

Maybe it's because she is playing hard to get and all guys like a good game of cat and mouse, but Mathieu believes, deep down, that this could be something more.

Now the only question is how to convince his realtor of all this.

The next day, Violette has chosen four more properties to show him. The first house is one that Mathieu immediately dislikes, but he doesn't admit this right away. He doesn't want to rush any of the home tours.

"What don't you like about it?" she asks.

"You should ask what I do like. That list is much shorter."

"Luc, be serious."

"Fine. I hate the location. It's much too busy for me. I despise the paint colors."

"Paint colors can be fixed," she interrupts.

"Do you know how many coats it will take to paint over that magenta room?"

"Three."

"You're kidding right now, aren't you?"

"I don't joke about paint colors."

"You don't joke about much, do you?"

"Okay, okay, so you hate the house. Moving along."

Mathieu finds her habit of changing the subject irritatingly charming, but he plays her game.

"So whatever happened with your date? Did that work out?"

"Oh, gosh, that was awful." Violette laughed. "We didn't even go on a date. I met the guy, he looked just like my boss, and it was just too strange."

"Shot down before he even got a chance! Poor guy!" Mathieu says, laughing and feeling pleased. The idea of her with any other guy makes him jealous, which he knows is ridiculous, but he can't help it.

"Which unlucky guy is the next to have his heart broken by Violette Deschamps?"

"I can't tell you that. It would be unprofessional."

Violette laughs as she runs her hand along a window.

With every minute that Mathieu spends with Violette, he finds himself more and more interested in her. This is a feeling so unlike the ones with any other woman he knows. There's an air of mystery about her. She's like a hidden gem that only he can see.

The second home is total fixer-upper, and he almost considers it until he knocks on a wall and part of it crumbles. They are out of that house so fast! Today's houses are all terrible.

Mathieu holds the door for Violette, and he loves feeling how close she is as she scoots by him, laughing. Her laughter is contagious.

When they're both outside, Violette admits that the house was not what she was expecting either.

"I should hope not! It needs new everything, walls, floors, ceiling."

Mathieu hopes she shows him many more houses that are this awful. For every awful house he sees, it means they have to go see another, which means more time with Violette. It also means he is getting closer to finding his dream home. Eventually, he will have to choose a home. One month or less, he reminds himself.

While the house is practically in ruins, the grounds far make up for the actual dwelling. They're in a private-park-like setting not too far from Paris. There is a river meandering through the back property, little currents with white tops rushing downstream in an even tempo.

"I figured it would be a long day, so I packed a lunch. Do you want to take a break? We can have a picnic by the river," Violette says.

"You did this for me?"

"Well, and me. I had to eat too!"

"Is it safe? I don't want the house to come crumbling down on us," he jokes, pleased with her gesture. "Do you do this for all your strikingly handsome clients?"

Violette laughs.

She seems to do this anytime she wants to divert a question from Mathieu.

Women are so complicated, he thinks.

She grabs the picnic supplies from the car and spreads out a red-and-white-checkered cloth on the ground then starts pulling out the food.

"This looks so good." Mathieu loves how generous and considerate she is. He helps her open up some of the containers filled with a fresh baguette, grapes, cheese, deli meats, and macaroons.

"You are a woman of many talents, Violette Deschamps," he says as he looks directly at her.

She looks shy all of the sudden as she hands him a plate.

"Are you doing all of this because you were so sad you missed dinner with me? You, Violette, rejected me. I'm hurt!" he jokes playfully and puts an imaginary dagger to his heart. He lies down on the picnic cloth and pretends to play dead.

"I didn't reject you! I really was busy."

"So does that mean we can have dinner sometime, just you and me?"

"Eat your lunch," Violette says coolly. "We still have two more properties to see."

They eat and talk and eat and talk some more. The time they spend on the lawn overlooking the river puts them a little behind schedule, but neither party seems to mind.

"This is heaven," Mathieu says.

Violette nods in agreement.

As they enjoy a leisurely lunch, they spend time getting to know one another. Violette remains professional, and Mathieu wishes she would lighten up just a little. He sees her as a friend, even though she still seems so guarded.

Out of nowhere, Mathieu, still lying on the picnic cloth, turns to his side and props his head up with hand.

"I can't stop thinking about you," he blurts out.

A comfortable pause exists between the pair, and he can tells Violette is surprised but not displeased.

He waits for her reaction.

He watches the inquisitive expression on her cute little face.

He looks at her expectantly, patiently.

And he is even more surprised by her response.

"I've thought about you too."

"Really?" He beams. "Good thoughts or bad?"

"Awful. I keep thinking what an indecisive client you are!" she jokes. "I'm kidding. Good thoughts."

"I like hearing that."

They exchange genuine smiles with one another.

"I actually told my mother about you," Violette says. "That came out on wrong," she says, cheeks reddening.

With kind eyes and a gentle tone, Mathieu asks, "What did she say? You can't say something like that and not divulge the secrets that were shared!"

"This is embarrassing."

"I think it's cute," he says flirtatiously. "So, don't make me keep asking. What did she say about me?"

Violette pauses, deep in thoughts.

"Violette?" he says in a singsong voice.

"My mother is very ill. She didn't know that I was even talking to her. Her body is still here, but her mind... her mind is already gone."

Violette talks openly about her mom, wishing that she hadn't. It's terribly unprofessional, yet it feels so good to have a person to talk to.

"I'm really sorry, Violette."

Mathieu feels for Violette and her loneliness. Here he is trying to escape for time alone, while it seems as though it's all this poor woman has. And he can truly empathize. He knows he would fall apart if he were facing the prospect of losing either his mother or his father. However, he would still have a giant support system in the form of brothers and sisters.

He wants to be Violette's support system. He wants to envelop her in a giant hug, hold her hand, or kiss her forehead, but he can tell she wants to drop the subject.

To lighten the mood, Mathieu tells her a little bit about his family and his siblings.

He tells her all about his parents, his hippie-painter mom. How opposite his father is and how he is a business consultant. He tells her about their home in Montmartre.

He tells her about his siblings, and he even tells her that Madeleine is his twin. He takes extra care to avoid revealing his real name.

He tells her about the vacations they would take growing up and the trouble he and his brothers would get in.

He tells her that his parents always encouraged all them to find out who they were and be their own person.

"I think it sounds wonderful," Violette says. "It's great you have such a big family. It sounds like a storybook."

For a moment, Mathieu wonders if it sounds as if he is gloating about his family. While they are far from perfect—no family is perfect—they have shaped who he had become.

"I'd love to see Madeleine again and meet the rest of your family." Violette puts a hand over her mouth, as if regretting what she said.

Mathieu only grins. "Nothing would make me happier."

He means it. Violette would fit in perfectly with the Deneuve clan. His parents would adore her. More importantly, Mathieu adores her.

He slices off a hunk of baguette. As he chews, he lets the idea soak in. He, Mathieu Deneuve, adores this woman. As she takes a sip of her drink, he watches her lips and thinks of how kissable they look and how she would smack him in the face if he tried a single move.

The mere thought of that makes him chuckle.

Violette doesn't say anything else. She smiles shyly at Mathieu and just enjoys the moment and bizarreness of it all. She likes this guy, he seems to like her back, and she allows herself to be happy, if only for the day. Once he buys his house, it will be back to normal, but for now, living in the moment is where she wants to be.

They lie there, listening to the river, looking at the clouds, munching on picnic leftovers, content bursts of silence between topics. Violette knows they need to keep moving on the house hunt, even though she would love to freeze this moment forever.

"Should we go?" she asks.

"Go where? Swimming?"

"In the river? Are you crazy?" she exclaims.

"Yes to both."

"No to the river," Violette says.

"Can we at least take a walk? I need to scope out the grounds and see if this is suitable for my future home."

Violette rolls her eyes at him.

"You hate this place," she teases.

"C'mon, let's go walk. Just for a moment, please?" he begs, then smiles slyly. "I need to fully investigate every inch of this property. As you are my realtor, I insist you accompany me."

She can't say no.

CHAPTER FIFTEEN

They leave their picnic remnants as is and stand up to make their way down the gentle slope toward the water's edge. Violette picks two tiny crumbs off her lap and counts the steps it takes to get there. Whenever Violette gets nervous, she counts. It's a habit that she has done ever since she was young. It takes them precisely sixty-eight steps to get to the bank of the river, not that she says this aloud.

Mathieu asks a couple of questions about the property line and how far it extends. They both know he does not care one bit about the answers, but Violette answers anyway.

As they are walking and talking, Mathieu suddenly comes to a halt and steps in front of Violette before turning to face her.

"Miss Violette Deschamps, will you please put me out of my misery and just tell me, is there really no one else in your life? Not even an ex you're still hung up on? I am going to stand here until you answer, and if you don't answer, we are going swimming. I don't joke about a good swim."

She looks him right in the eye. "Luc Deneuve, really, I don't have anyone in my life. Or a cat I might add. Thank you for reminding me."

"I'm not sure I believe you."

"Believe it. Trust me, I'm telling you the truth."

Her answer satisfies him for the moment, although he's not sure he believes her. Why did she reject him then? Millions of girls think he is a catch.

The river extends a long way through the property, but Violette isn't entirely sure where the lines cross over to the next person's land. Neither of them seems to have any intention of turning back just yet.

They walk slowly, the pace of a light stroll, and they walk close to one another, side by side. They aren't touching, but they are both acutely aware of their proximity to one another. Mathieu debates whether or not he should make a move, albeit a small one, and smoothly grab her hand.

Not being one to avoid risks, he goes for it.

When Violette's arm swings back naturally as she walks, Mathieu lightly grabs one of her fingers. Inch by inch, he holds her petite, delicate hand a little tighter.

She doesn't give much of a reaction, but she doesn't object either.

Well, this is a good start, Mathieu thinks. He swears he sees her face flush with a hint of color.

He squeezes her hand, and she squeezes back, the corners of her lips turning up with a slight smile.

"Do you want to sit?" she asks him.

"Sure. This is a good place just to soak in the view."

She doesn't object when he motions for her to sit on a tree stump. He sits on the ground beside her.

"I'm going to tell you a secret," he says matter-of-factly.

"Okay, I like secrets."

"I think you are my muse." He says this in such a serious tone that Violette can't help but let a giggle escape.

"Your muse?"

She realizes that he is being serious.

"I'm not joking. I need to keep you around."

"Shall I charge commission on my muse services?" she says.

Mathieu lets out a sigh, but not one full of irritation as he had been doing so frequently just weeks before.

"Okay, I'll be serious." She musters up her best serious facial expression, which makes Mathieu burst into laughter. He takes his hand and gently pats her leg.

"I love to sing, and I love to play the guitar." He leaves out the whole famed musician thing since she hasn't picked up on it yet. He knows she'll find out eventually and will probably be mad that he lied about his name. It's a chance he is still willing to take.

"I even write my own lyrics."

"That's so cool, Luc."

"Well, I had been struggling to formulate any songs that I truly loved. I had ideas. I'd sit down to write them out. I would make notes everywhere I went, but nothing. Then I met you."

Violette looks at him patiently, waiting for him to continue. She plays with a strand of grass sprouting up from beside the stump, rubbing it between her fingers.

"Violette, it all changed when I met you. Lyrics came rushing to me, and I feel as if my music is coming alive again."

She isn't sure what to say. She is incredibly flattered to be the inspiration of his songs, but she feels slightly disappointed that maybe he doesn't like her, he just likes the reaction she has on his music. She tries to brush that thought aside, but it nags her.

"Care to share?" she asks, genuinely hoping to hear a snippet of a Luc Deneuve song.

"Absolutely," he says.

He pretends to strum a few chords on his air guitar and hums the opening sounds, a cappella style. The melody is much slower, much softer than that of his previous songs.

Words start to tumble across his lips, as he sings the lyrics to a song about a girl who came into his life and made him feel alive.

Violette thinks his voice is beautiful, edgy, yet romantic, breathy, and strong. When he is done, he takes Violette by both hands and pulls her up from the tree stump where she has been sitting. Their bodies are close to one another, facing each other, their hands touching.

Mathieu, who stands about a head taller than Violette, begins to lower his head to one side, and Violette knows he is trying to kiss her. If she turns her head up, she knows their lips will touch. She knows they'll share their first kiss.

In a split-second decision, Violette takes a small, subtle step backward. It's enough to give Mathieu the message; it's a message he is surprised to receive.

He releases her hands, and an awkward tension floats between them. They both recognize what almost happened, and they both recognize what the other one wanted.

Violette breaks the silence. "So we should probably start heading back. We still have two more properties to see, and I don't want us to miss our appointments."

"Yes, that would be a tragedy," Mathieu says. It sounds more aloof that he intends.

Then in a serious, grave tone, he takes both her hands and faces her. "I need to tell you something." In a split-second decision, Mathieu decides to share he is really Mathieu, despite the bad timing.

Violette's vivid imagination kicks in again. They are alone by the river, with no one around. Is he about to tell her he's a serial killer? Violette panics, looking for an escape route and recalling from her psychology class she once took that serial killers seem so nice and friendly at first impression. Or was that a different personality disorder? She wishes she could remember.

Her expression must be one of fear, because he instantly tries to make her feel better.

"It's nothing that bad. Don't worry."

"Okay."

"My name isn't really Luc."

Violette is really panicking now. Why didn't they cover cute clients who take you down to the river's edge alone in Real Estate 101? Oh wait, that's simply common sense.

How could you be so stupid? Violette thinks. She turns to walk back to the car. *This is bad, Violette, this is bad.*

As amused as Mathieu is to see her panic, he runs after her.

"Violette, stop. I'm still Madeleine's brother. My real name is Mathieu, Mathieu Deneuve."

She does stop, but she's a safer distance from the river now.

"Why did you tell me it was Luc?"

She looks angry. He knows he should have told her earlier, but how do you tell someone you really like that you aren't who they think you are?

"Mathieu Deneuve?" She looks skeptical.

"That's me."

"How am I supposed to believe you?"

"Please, Violette, I'm telling the truth." He grabs her hand, and she pulls it away.

He pulls out his wallet and shows her his credit cards and passport, which all clearly have his name printed: Mathieu Deneuve.

She relaxes a little.

"Why didn't you tell me? Why did you say you were Luc? Why did you lie to me?"

"I didn't lie. It wasn't intentional."

Mathieu doesn't know if he should go ahead and come clean about being the lead singer for Les Slinks. She doesn't seem to recognize the name.

"Luc's a nickname," he says, trying to pull this off smoothly.

"Oh, well then why did you make a big deal about this?"

"I'm not sure." He laughs sheepishly. "Can we forget it? I just needed a realtor but didn't want to deal with my connection to Madeleine."

Violette feels as though there is more to the story, but she doesn't know what to ask, except, "So should I call you Luc or Mathieu?"

"Either. Mathieu is good though."

As they walk back up the car, with the sweet moment shared between them ruined, they both agree on one thing: something is weird and complicated between them.

They trace their same steps in reverse, heading back to clean up their picnic dishes, both lost in their own thoughts.

Violette feels appalled at her behavior and vows to keep things more professional from here on out. This is a big client, and she is representing the entire Domaines D'Elegance office. She can't let Jean-Philippe down. As they walk in silence, she tells herself not to make a big deal out of something that didn't happen. A kiss that almost happened is still a kiss that didn't happen.

Nothing happened, Vi, she says to herself again.

But why didn't she let it happen? Luc or Mathieu, or whoever he is, is surprising sweet. And incredibly handsome. What's wrong with her? She's been alone for so long that she's gotten used to it. Is she so afraid to be happy again?

Mathieu, walking right beside her, is having his own thoughts. *It's just a kiss, dude,* he tells himself. He's kissed dozens and dozens of girls before, some of them not meaning a thing. *It's no big deal, it's no big deal,* he repeats to himself. Besides, Violette doesn't seem to be making a big deal of it. She doesn't even seem to care. Maybe she didn't notice? But he knows that is not the truth.

Instead, Mathieu begins to think that Violette is a tease, maybe a prude.

As they get in the car, Mathieu decides that he is just bold enough to ask the questions that are sometimes better left unspoken.

"Violette," he starts. She turns to look at him. "This next question, it is none of my business, but I'm going to ask anyway. Please forgive me in advance if this offends you."

This piques her interest.

"Violette." He says her name again. "Are you the type of woman who leads men on? You flirt with them, you bat your pretty eyes at them, you let them sing to you, and then when they try to kiss you, you are just like, 'Oh, never mind'?"

She is floored by his question, and she picks up the anger, or maybe it's sadness, that she detects in his voice. His accusatory question and the fact that he just assumes that Violette behaves in such a way angers her, and he can tell.

"That may have been a little out of line. I'm sorry, Violette."

She nods her head as a peace offering and doesn't give an answer to this question because she isn't sure what to say. She doesn't think what he is saying is true, but she certainly does not want him to think of her as someone who toys with emotions. She doesn't dangle the carrot and then just take it away. But for goodness sake, she thinks, doesn't he realize that this is her job? She is being paid to sell homes, not kiss her clients on romantic strolls by the river!

As they walk through the third home of the day, which Mathieu doesn't hate but doesn't love, they are cordial to one another. Violette does a fine job of pointing out the home's flaws, selling points, and additional commentary.

Mathieu wishes that he could take back his question. He knows it was inappropriate, too forward, too personal, too everything wrong. He's worried that he has messed things up with Violette before he ever even has a chance with her. And he is livid with himself, anger and irritation flooding into his veins.

Finally, as they walk into the fourth house, they are upstairs touring through what appears to be a sitting room or an office space, Violette decides to break the tension.

"Listen, I'm sorry about before. I'm not that kind of girl, and I don't want you to have that kind of impression of me."

The anger and irritation from Mathieu slowly thins.

"Then, Violette, have dinner with me. This weekend. Please?"

Shyly, Violette nods her head yes. Mathieu grabs her right hand with both of his and gives it a squeeze. Then he kisses the top of her hand.

"Finally!" he says, doing a little victory dance.

CHAPTER SIXTEEN

*O*f the four people sitting in the dim club in the middle of the day, only one of them is happy: Adrien Henri. He has rented out the Black Light nightclub for the afternoon so they can hold auditions for the role of the new front man for Les Slinks. All the band members, except for Mathieu, are present, but this is the last place they want to be.

Adrien senses the low morale of the group.

"Guys, this is going to be fun. I know Mathieu is your main guy and your friend, but seriously, give this a chance. We're going to find a new, improved lead singer." He stops to scratch his chin, and then stands up, slaps his fist to the small bar table and announces with great enthusiasm, "This new guy will be Mathieu Deneuve, but better."

The guys groan and roll their eyes.

"If we have to sit through this crap," Oliver says, "can we at least get some beer from the bar?"

Guillaume and Marcel nod in agreement, looking like eager schoolboys.

"Oh, all right," Adrien agrees, but he isn't happy about it. He knows he has to give in somewhere.

He snaps his fingers, and one of the Black Light employees comes over and takes their orders.

Adrien obnoxiously climbs up the two stairs to the small stage and in his booming voice welcomes Les Slinks.

"Dude, we are the only ones here," Guillaume says, taking a sip of beer from his frosty mug.

"Yeah, can you skip this whole show and just get on with the first act?" Marcel asks.

"We are building up hype for the new guys in the back," Adrien whispers.

"Well, we don't care about the dog-and-pony show. Just bring out contestant number one," Olivier says mockingly and as if he were on a game show on television.

"Fine," Adrien says. "The first guy is a young man named Marc." In a hushed tone, he adds, "His name even starts with an M, just like Mathieu."

"We can all spell here, Adrien," Guillaume says.

"Just bring him on stage already," Marcel says.

Marc comes on stage, and he looks nothing like Mathieu, but even the guys can admit that he is handsome.

"I'm Marc, and this song is dedicated to Adrien. Thanks for bringing me to the audition, man." He points to Adrien, the band shakes their head in disgust, and Marc begins to strum on the guitar.

Based on the guitar skills, the band is mildly impressed.

Then he started singing.

It is painful. He is so horrible, so awful, that Marcel cuts him off before he is done.

"Thank you, Marc," he says. "We are looking for something very specific. That will be all."

Marc looks disappointed and slinks off stage.

"Okay, maybe he wasn't the best choice," Adrien says. "But we have a full list of auditions. One guy down, twenty to go."

"Joy," Olivier says with great sarcasm.

The next guy can sing and play the guitar. He's incredible, actually, they can all admit to that. The look just isn't there. He doesn't have the wow factor in terms of handsomeness. He's cute in a boy-next-door kind of way. Blond hair, khaki pants, a polo shirt. He looks as if he could be a model in a department store catalog. Cute and sweet isn't quite the look of Mathieu Deneuve. This guy wouldn't make all the girls swoon. In this industry, that matters.

The third guy is just okay. He can sing and even has the raspy voice. However, his stage performance is timid, weak. Les Slinks needs someone dynamic and wild, someone who can feel the crowd's energy and respond to it in a way that pumps up the fans even more.

The next performer comes on. Followed by the next, and the next, and the next.

And fortunately, as the day goes on, some of the singers are good, great actually. Yet the three band members always, always find something wrong with him or, in two cases, her. Too short, not enough stage presence, guitar skills mediocre, too clean cut, too punk. None of them meet the standards for any of them, and Adrien is just plain frustrated and fed up with the whole lot.

Yet he knows they are right. Adrien or Les Slinks cannot put just anyone up on the big stage.

Not every performer can make arenas sell out and achieve international fame. Mathieu can. The guys auditioning at the Black Light can't. This is the front man. He has to be perfect, especially if Adrien wants to spring for an even bigger place perched on the Mediterranean Sea. They just need to keep looking.

What we need, Adrien thinks, *is someone who has a voice similar to Mathieu's signature raspy tenor, and we need for this person to look twice as nice.* He's out there, Adrien is sure of it.

He is also sure that he desperately needs to boost the morale of the band, stat, especially after overhearing their conversation.

"Face it, guys, we are doomed."

"This sucks."

"I think we should start looking for new careers."

Adrien, always being the man with a plan, quickly interjects.

"I don't like this talk one bit," he says, wagging his finger at the three. With exasperation in his voice, he carries on. "No one is getting a new job, just a promotion and raise when you see that my plan will work. I have said this before, and I will probably have to tell you this many times more: Mathieu is a traitor to all of you. If he cared about you or the band he wouldn't have put you in this situation. If he cared about his career, he would have asked for time off and kept you three, and me, in the loop."

He pauses to take a deep breath in, pacing in front of the guys.

"But did Mathieu do any of that? No. Mathieu disappeared. And I am looking out for you, Guillaume. And you, Marcel. And you, Olivier."

With a nod of satisfaction, Adrien awaits their reactions.

Marcel, the most outspoken of the three mumbles, "I feel like a traitor still."

The other two shrug their shoulders, not wanting to agree with either Marcel or Adrien.

"Remember, you three, Mathieu is the traitor here, the Judas. He is the one who didn't take your livelihood into consideration. I'm just trying to pick up the pieces and put them back together." He gestures with his hands as if he were actually working on a puzzle.

They sit at the bar talking in the Black Lights room, just the four of them, long after the last performer has gone home. One beer after another, no one is feeling hopeful.

Finally, at one point, Adrien looks them each right in the eye. "Guys, a real friend would at least have the decency to keep in touch."

Adrien thinks his words are working, that he is truly convincing the guys that Mathieu is the villain here, the diva who feels he has grown too big for his band.

Once the band realizes it, the auditions will go so much better since they will want to replace their beloved Mathieu. He's tempted to let out an evil laugh. Maybe he can even buy a yacht.

Adrien has been doing most of the talking, and none of the band members are surprised. Marcel finally gets a word in. "I have tried to get in touch with Mathieu."

"Unsuccessfully, I assume?" Olivier asks.

"Obviously. He's not here, and we are."

Adrien sees how snippy they are with one another and surprisingly just lets them talk, while he listens... a rarity.

Guillaume, the quietest one of the bunch, asks them, "Do you think he's coming back? Or do you think he really deserted us?"

"There is no telling with that dude," Olivier says, taking a sip of his beer and leaning on the bar. "But this is a little extreme, even for him.

I think there is a fifty-fifty chance he's coming back."

"Wanna flip a coin? Heads he is coming back, tails he's outta here for good." Guillaume takes a euro coin out of his pocket. "You call it," he says, nodding to Olivier.

"Heads."

Guillaume flips the coin. It's tails.

"Crap," Guillaume says. "I think he's out."

Olivier agrees. "I do too."

Adrien adds to the conversation to boost the camaraderie. "You're both right."

Marcel, on the other hand, rebuts this notion. "You are wrong. All of you. He said he would be back in two months. It hasn't been two months. Have a little faith in him." He pauses. "I think he'll be back in time to start developing the next album. Don't give up hope. Not yet, at least."

Silence floods the Black Light Bar.

Marcel has had enough. "I'm outta here."

***

A couple of days pass since the first round of auditions, which even Adrien admits did not go so well. He promised the guys he would find their Mathieu replacement in six weeks, and he wants to hold true to that promise. He hates breaking promises, and he wants to get the new band moving as soon as possible. Adrien refuses to give up hope.

Since the band is as excited and enthusiastic about holding live auditions as they would be attending the funeral of a complete stranger, Adrien decides to take a different approach. The new approach gives him more control and power over the whole situation, which Adrien is elated about.

He puts together an eye-catching ad and carefully chooses some of the best photos of the band from some of their biggest touring gigs. Satisfied with the end result, he posts it to a website where up-and-coming musicians can post about themselves and where record execs can search for new talent. It's kind of like Internet dating sites, but for the music industry.

His brilliant idea is to send out a call for video auditions. He can weed out the ones he doesn't like, narrow down his selections, and then let Les Slinks choose from his list of appropriate choices. He laughs. *Why didn't I think of this sooner?*

Now, all he has to do is sit back and watch the videos roll in like a gigantic tidal wave.

Things are looking up, up, up for me! Adrien says to himself with a smile plastered on his unruly face.

CHAPTER SEVENTEEN

*W*hen Marcel flees the Black Light, he hails a taxicab. Once inside, he pulls out his cell phone and types an e-mail addressed to Madeleine. He can't let Mathieu just be replaced. He and Mathieu were the founding fathers of Les Slinks. Mathieu got Olivier to join, and then discovering Guillaume completed their masterpiece.

It doesn't change the fact that Marcel is livid with Mathieu. But he could never forgive himself if he didn't at least try everything to get in touch with his friend. After all, if Marcel was in Mathieu's place, he knows Mathieu would fight for him. Madeleine just might be Marcel's lifeline.

Hey, Madeleine,

Hope all is well wherever you are! I know you talk to that twin of yours, and I am desperate to get in touch him with. So much is going on, and Mathieu needs to be in touch with me ASAP...or risk being kicked out of Les Slinks. I need to know where he is and he's not answering my texts, calls or emails. Please, Mad? Even if he says he doesn't want to bothered, this is bigger than his immediate desire. Phone number, secret e-mail he's using, where he is staying, anything, any leads, would be much appreciated.

Thanks!

—Marcel

Madeleine gets the message a few moments after Marcel hits send. She is in between set changes and only has a minute to glance at her inbox. She briefly questions whether or not she should give out the number he gave her, but decides it sounds important enough to break twin code.

Seeing that the set isn't quite ready, she runs back to her trailer and looks for the slip of paper with the Mathieu's number on it. She looks in her pants pocket. She checks the pockets of a few other pairs of pants. Nothing. She checks her suitcase and desk, and she shakes some papers to see if it falls out. Not there.

Where could it be? she wonders. *Think, Madeleine.*

She looks in every drawer, every nook, and every cranny of her trailer on set.

There are no signs of this paper.

Madeleine starts to panic. Mathieu trusted her with this info, and now, what if no one can find him? Ever?

She knows she has to get back to work. They are already behind production schedule and don't have a minute to waste.

She crafts a quick response to Marcel.

Marcel,

Good to hear from you! I have been in touch with Mathieu, but lost the number he gave me. Ugh, I wish I could find it. Busy on set, will let you know the minute I find it. Don't worry, Mathieu will show back up. No one can control my evil twin!

—Madeleine

On her short walk back to set, she calls the only one who can drop everything and hunt

Mathieu down thanks to his flexible schedule: Xavier.

Xavier is the second-youngest Deneuve clan member, and when Madeleine calls him, he is at the gym, which doesn't surprise her a bit. He is fresh out of university, and he's pursuing a career in boxing.

In between rounds of hitting the punching bag, he hears his phone ring. Normally he would silence it. However, when he sees the call is coming from Madeleine, he picks it up in an instant. She rarely calls, especially when she's in a different country for work.

"Hey, Mad." He answers the phone, hoping everything is okay. "Are you calling to give me a hard time about my mohawk again?"

"Actually, I need your help."

"What's going on?"

"Mathieu is missing in action. He gave me his number to his secret hideout spot, but I can't find it. I'm still in Prague, and I got an alarming message from Marcel. He needs to get in touch with our daredevil of a brother. Can you track him down?"

"Seriously, Mad? Can't we just let him do his thing? You know Mathieu."

"Xavier," she says in a warning voice, "I think something big is happening. Something with his band. Mathieu was acting weird, and I just think we need to find him."

"Fine. I'm almost done with my session here. The second I'm done, I'm outta here."

"Okay. Thanks, Xavier! And start at my house. He hung out there for a few days."

"I'll keep ya posted! Later, sis."

"Oh, and Xavier?"

"Yeah?"

"Thanks."

The things you do for family, Xavier thinks as he puts his phone back in the corner of the gym beside the sweaty towel he just used to wipe his face.

As he goes back to working on his hooks, he feels more momentum, motivation. As much as he loves his family and all his siblings, they can be so incredibly frustrating. There's always some sort of crisis and he's not the kind of guy who likes drama. However, he would do anything for them. He lets out a powerful punch right to the sweet spot of the punching bag.

After his morning training session and shower at the gym, he goes over to Madeleine's apartment. He knows the code of the front entrance by heart and gets in the building easily. On the second floor, he looks above the hallway light for her spare key. When she first told him where the spare key was hidden, he couldn't help but give her a hard time.

"On top of the lamp, really?" He was incredulous. That has to be the first place that burglars and thieves look for an easy way into a home. Especially as a single girl living alone!

Xavier finds the key and lets himself in. If Mathieu had indeed been here, he sure kept the place clean. The kitchen is spotless. The beds are all made up. Nothing is out of place. Xavier feels like a crook trying to find the valuables and riches as he hunts around the house for any traces of Mathieu, or hints as to where he could be.

On a whim, Xavier opens up the trash can. Empty. As he closes the lid, a small business card at the bottom catches his eye. He dumpster dives and retrieves the single piece of paper, which just happens to be a business card for Domaines D'Elegance.

Mathieu house hunting? It's his only lead. If he calls, what would he say? "Um, hi, my name is Xavier, and I'm trying to find my grown adult brother?" He slips the card, thankfully clean, in his pocket and keeps searching the house.

He uses Madeleine's phone to call Marcel, Olivier, and Guillaume. Marcel's phone goes to voicemail, and no good information comes from his quick conversations with Olivier and Guillaume.

He locks the front door and places the spare key back over the light.

He drives by Mathieu's apartment and knocks on the door but gets no response. After that, he shuttles around Paris to the places Mathieu hangs out and checks in on a couple of diners, the gym, and a few bars. It's too early for the bars though. He knows that going in, but anything at this point is worth trying.

"Mathieu, where are you?" Xavier says aloud.

He decides to give Domaines D'Elegance a visit. He has a hunch and no other viable options.

He pulls up to the address on the card and walks in. Brigitte immediately greets him.

"Thank you for visiting Domaines D'Elegance. My name is Brigitte. How can I help you today?" she asks.

"Hello. This is a peculiar question, and I am well aware of that. My name is Xavier Deneuve, and I am looking for my brother. I'm Madeleine Deneuve's brother, I think she did some business with you guys for a while. Like

I said, I know this sounds crazy. His name is Mathieu Deneuve—from Les Slinks. Have you heard from him? Seen him?"

Brigitte is dumbfounded and isn't sure how best to handle this peculiar request.

"Sir, I'm a huge fan of Les Slinks, but no Mathieu has been working with us. However..." Brigitte pauses.

"However, what?" Xavier asks.

"Let me have you speak to my supervisor. Hang on, sir."

She pages Jean-Philippe's number and asks him to come up to the front. After all, Violette's newest client requested the utmost discretion in all matters of the case.

"Jean-Philippe, proprietor of Domaines D'Elegance." He extends his hand, and Xavier shakes it.

"Hi, Jean-Philippe, my name is Xavier Deneuve, one of Madeleine's brothers."

"Another Deneuve?" Jean-Philippe exclaims brightly. "Your family is wonderful. How can Domaines D'Elegance be of assistance?"

"I'm actually looking for my brother, Mathieu."

"Mathieu?" Jean-Philippe asks.

"You sound surprised, sir."

Jean-Philippe *is* surprised, and despite the discretion requested, he has to watch out for his realtors, especially Violette, who he sees as practically a daughter.

"There seems to be a bit of a mistake," Jean-Philippe says. "Why don't you tell me what's going on, and I'll see if I can help you."

Xavier pauses. Jean-Philippe stares at him, waiting.

"Mathieu Deneuve, my brother, has gone missing. He's the lead singer of the band Les Slinks. Madeleine was in touch with him briefly. He stayed at her house. However, she was out of town."

"I'm with you so far," Jean-Philippe says.

Xavier continues, "I found a card for your business at her house. I'm trying to follow any potential leads, and so here I am, talking to you, trying to figure out where he might be."

Jean-Philippe hates breaking client privacy, and he isn't quite ready to do so now. However, he will absolutely be doing an internal investigation. "I can say with full certainty that we do not have a customer named Mathieu Deneuve right now."

"Thank you for your time," Xavier says.

Always the businessman, Jean-Philippe adds, "But if we can assist with any home-buying or selling needs, please be sure to let us know. We're the best in France!"

Xavier tries not to roll his eyes. They say their good-byes, each more puzzled than they were before the conversation took place.

So much for that lead, Xavier thinks, although both Brigitte and the supervisor seem to be acting a little suspicious.

"Mathieu, where are you?" he mutters aloud again for the umpteenth time today.

Brigitte excitedly says to Jean-Philippe, "I love Les Slinks! I didn't know they were all related. What a talented family."

"Yes, but something weird is going on," Jean-Philippe responds before hastily walking back to his office and shutting the door. Luc or Mathieu, Jean-Philippe will get down to the bottom of this.

CHAPTER EIGHTEEN

*X*avier is completely befuddled about where Mathieu is hiding. He's frustrated, and he knows Madeleine will be as well.

You certainly win at hide-and-seek, Xavier thinks as he walks down the street, trying to figure out if he can come up with any more leads.

So far, zilch!

Little does he know, as he is walking past the bistro, the one and only Violette Deschamps walks past Xavier.

Unaware of whom she just passed, Violette walks up the steps to the office. When she enters into the building, Brigitte immediately jumps up from her desk.

Brigitte gets excited over everything from the latest nail polish trends to hearing her favorite song on the radio to throwing giant parties for the smallest of holidays.

Upon hearing her in the office, Jean-Philippe comes out of his own office to join in on Brigitte's commotion. Since no clients are in the office, they talk openly.

"When you were out of the office, a man came in looking for a guy named Mathieu Deneuve, saying they were both brothers of Madeleine. Does any of this sound familiar to you?" Jean-Philippe asks her.

"Nope, not really," Violette says, keeping her answers vague. For whatever reason, she genuinely trusts Mathieu. The way he talks about his family, his lyrics. He's gentle underneath the moody, temperamental beast. Violette has actually noticed that he seems to be becoming less and less irritated with every meeting they have. *Maybe I really am his muse*, she thinks to herself.

"Violette, do you know who Mathieu Deneuve is?" Brigitte asks, clearly astonished that she isn't getting more of a reaction from her friend.

"No," she says.

"Mathieu Deneuve? Lead singer of Les Slinks? Please tell me you know the band Les Slinks."

"Never heard of them."

"Violette, seriously?! They are only the hottest band in Paris, and they've toured internationally! You are kidding me, right?"

"I'm not kidding," she says seriously.

"We have got to get you out more," Brigitte says, shaking her head in pure amazement.

"Promise me, you will at least look them up. The Internet is a world of knowledge, my friend."

"Sure," Violette says, although they both know she won't. She never has understood the whole infatuation with actors and actresses and musicians and celebrities. They're just people, but maybe that's because she grew up with old-fashioned parents who didn't get the entertainment industry. The Deschamps didn't even have a TV. Perhaps that's why Violette is such an avid reader with a wild imagination.

"There's nothing to worry about, guys," Violette says as she heads to her office to get started for the day.

She doesn't know what is going on with Mathieu, but for once, she feels content not to have all the answers or a crystal glass ball to predict the future. One thing she is certain of is that she likes the direction of these new beginnings.

Not long after she starts checking her emails, Brigitte informs her that her clients are in for their morning appointment. She walks to the front with Brigitte to greet them.

"Clara, Jared, nice to see you. Are you guys excited to get the keys to your new house on La Rue de Baie today?"

"So excited!" Clara gushes. "The first room we are decorating is for the baby."

"But I'm not going to see it until after the baby is born," Jared adds.

"You aren't helping?" Violette gives him a scolding, playful look.

"He doesn't want to know the sex of the baby, but I couldn't not know. He put together the furniture and as soon as we get the keys, a friend is coming to paint."

"It'll be more fun to wait, I think." Jared adds. "I tried to convince her to go with a gender-neutral theme, but she is stubborn, my Clara."

These two just radiate love for each other. *Something this perfect breaks eventually, right?*

Violette thinks, hating that the thought crossed her mind.

"Well, come on back, and let's get your signatures on the paperwork so that baby can get his or her room." Violette waves them to follow her to the conference room.

A giant stack of paper awaits the Gardiniers. All that is between their dream home and the keys is tackling the mound of documents.

As they sign document after document, Violette is reminded of why she loves working with first-time homeowners. So much dreaming goes into finding that perfect first home, an experience unlike any other. Second-time homebuyers, on the other hand, aren't quite as dreamy eyed. They know what they want and what they don't want. They know the stresses of water leaks, broken appliances, home repairs, and weather damage.

In a way, working with the Gardiniers is like working with eager toddlers, seeing the world of real estate for the first time. It's great fun. Pens scratch on the paper, the final document is signed, and before she knows it, she pulls out an envelope.

"Congratulations, guys. You two are official-ly homeowners at La Rue de Baie!"

She hands them the envelope. Clara gives her a hug and whispers in her ear, "It's a girl!"

Violette smiles and is genuinely thrilled for them. A new home and a new baby—talk about some excitement! Clara is about seven months along, and they should have just enough time to get settled before Baby Girl Gardinier arrives.

The couple beams and leaves Domaines D'Elegance as homeowners. As with all of Violette's clients, they'll arrive to their new residence and be greeted with a vase of freshly cut flowers from Violette's favorite street vendor and a bottle of champagne. For the Gardiniers, she left sparkling cider instead, along with a heartfelt note wishing them the best of memories in their new home.

After her meeting with Clara and Jared, she jumps into making phone calls to another client who should close on a home next week. With the commissions of the recent sales, she should have enough left to splurge on some material for a few DIY projects she has wanted to do for quite a while.

Her stream of thought about the DIY plans is cut short when her cell phone rings. She smiles when she sees that it's Mathieu's name lighting up the screen. However, it still says Luc. She makes a mental note to change that and answers with a friendly hello.

"How's my favorite real estate agent doing today?" the voice on the other end of the line asks.

"I'm good. I'm catching up on a few things and checking in with some of my other clients."

"Sounds exhilarating," he says sarcastically. "I was calling today because I wanted to remind you of an extraspecial appointment with your extraspecial client tomorrow night. Are we still on for our date tomorrow?"

Violette feels her stomach flutter at the mention of the word *date*.

"Let me check my calendar. Yep, I have you penciled in between Eric and Luc."

"Very funny."

"I don't joke about dates."

"So you are in agreement with me. This is a date, not a professional meeting."

"It's a date, Mathieu."

"All right, I'll pick you up at your place. See you tomorrow."

As she hangs up the phone, she recalls their borderline flirtatious banter simply because it makes her so happy to think of it.

She hums as she sends e-mails, and before she knows it, the day is already almost over.

She has long forgotten the stranger looking for Mathieu, although she has a hunch there is more to his story than she immediately knows. It's like reading the mystery novels she loves so much, only a real-life version with a guy she really trusts. *The pages will unfold in time*, she tells herself.

After the workday, Violette does what she does every single night. She drives over to the hospice to see her mom.

Nadine is one of the night nurses on staff and lets her in.

"Something seems different about you. You seem happier."

"Same old thing every day," Violette says.

"Mmmhmmm," Nadine murmurs, not believing Violette one bit. "Is there a new leading man in your life?"

"Working on it," Violette says with a laugh.

"It's about time!" Nadine says, clapping her hands together as if she were in church. "Have a good visit with your mom," she adds as Violette makes her way down the long, winding corridor.

"Thanks."

When she gets down to her mother's room, the lights are all off, including the bedside table lamp, which should stay on at all times. Violette makes a mental note to say something to the staff.

Tonight, she skips fixing her mother's hair, but takes the time to read. They start a new mystery novel, one that she picked up at the library. As she starts to read, she can't help but feel like how her own life is a mystery novel. The last few weeks have truly shown her that you never know what is coming next. The good, the bad—there is always something lurking behind the present moment.

She stops reading midchapter and shares that thought with her mom, her sweet, frail, mother. So much of her mother's life is a mystery to Violette. There are so many stories that are untold, dreams not pursued, loves not requited. Hopes and aspirations and secrets abound in each person. She wishes desperately for more time with Lydia.

"Mom, I can't help but think my own story is being written. I feel as though I have a real shot with Mathieu. It's too early to tell, but I feel as if this might be the real thing. Life is turning around for me."

Her mother smiles in her sleep.

"I wish you could be here to see it all unfold," she whispers as she puts down the book and starts humming. Without realizing it, she is humming the song that Mathieu sang to her by the river. She may not know the words, but that melody will never be forgotten. It's forever engrained in her heart.

She hums the song all the way down the hallway and all the way home, where she opens up her closet to carefully choose something to wear tomorrow for her date with Mathieu. She is going for a look that is fun, flirty, but still Violette.

CHAPTER NINETEEN

*B*etween the home closing on La Rue de Baie with the Gardiniers and the closing next week for Cynthia DeFleurs, an older lady who recently lost her husband and is in the process of downsizing, Violette honestly hasn't done as much research as she should for the properties she is showing Mathieu today. She spent more time thinking about their date and less time thinking about his future home.

Maybe it's subconscious. Once Mathieu buys a house, the only way she'll get to see him is if they start dating and become something more. One date is clearly a good start, but what comes after one date? Another date? What if nothing comes after?

The minute Mathieu pick her up in front of the Domaines D'Elegance office, right on time, she stops her game of overanalyzing the details and turns to wing it with Mathieu. He hired a car and a driver because he didn't want her driving all the time, which Violette thought was silly, but she obliged to please him. They have four more properties to see, and as usual, they are all completely different in style. As cute as Mathieu is, Violette really does think he is a pain when it comes to buying a house. She doesn't mind though. She just wants to be a good real estate agent for him.

Violette herself is actually excited to see this first property on today's agenda. She has eyed it from the beginning of their search, and she knows it's a house she would love to live in. It's the Tuscan-inspired cottage with the angled rooflines and huge fields of wildflowers. And she swears she has seen this house in her dreams as they pull into the driveway. This house, this home, it is truly love at first sight for Violette. Too bad she isn't the one looking.

"This place is incredible!" Mathieu exclaims, shocking Violette.

"It's spectacular," she agrees.

Normally, Violette tries to keep her personal comments to a minimum or nonexistent when she is out with clients, but she can't help it.

She's human. And this house, this cottage is remarkable. It isn't a giant house, like some of the estates they have seen. It's small and totally charming. Bright-red shutters against the two-toned tan stucco and thatched roof shingles. Violette wishes she could stay forever, but again, that is not up to her.

But, oh, the projects! This place is begging for attention to detail, the perfect decorations, and a slew of do-it-yourself projects.

"Let's have a look, shall we?" she says.

She opens the door, and the minute that Mathieu walks in, she can tell this is his house. She can always tell when clients find their homes. They get starry looks in their eyes, they pause, and then they proceed to gush about every little detail. Every single time that this happens, she toys with the idea of writing a thesis and publishing it. The name of her article would be "Finding Your Dream Home: When Science and Emotions Collide."

"Violette, this place is awesome. I want it. I want to buy it right now."

This is music to any real estate agent's ears, but of course, she is practical.

"Well, look at the rest of it first!"

"Oh, I will, but this is my new home. I'll pay all cash for it right now. Can we do it?"

All cash deals in the real estate market are possible in a short period of time.

"Mathieu," she says gently, "there are also home inspections that need to be done."

"Violette, listen to me. I want this house. I love the land, the vibe, the house. This is my new home. I want it right now. Nothing is stopping me. Don't try to talk me out of it."

And she doesn't.

"It will still take a while to get this processed. Deals don't happen instantly. We need to negotiate the price and..."

Mathieu cuts her off.

"I'll pay full asking price. I just want this house immediately."

"That's crazy. No one offers full asking price."

"Then call me crazy."

That she will.

"Mathieu, stop."

He does stop, and he turns to look at her.

"Will you sleep on it? Decide in the morning?"

"No. I know what I like. Make it happen for me, Vi. Please?"

She sighs. Just because she hates rushing into big decisions doesn't mean that everyone else does. Her job is to cater to her clients and their home demands.

"All right, but don't expect this to happen instantly. There is a process."

"Let's not waste another second then!" he exclaims.

Violette grabs her phone to call the listing agent, where she informs him that her client wants to pay full asking price, all cash.

While they are waiting on the verbal offer to be accepted, their car drops Violette off at the office.

Before getting out of the car, she asks Mathieu one more time, "Are you sure you don't want to see the other properties lined up for the day? Just in case?"

Of course he says no, and she starts drawing up the paperwork. When the agent calls back and says they have a deal, she gets the contract ready for Mathieu.

They meet at the bistro for a quick lunch to sign the contract and go over the fine print. Mathieu could care less about the fine print. He just knows he wants the house.

Since the deal is all cash with no inspection, everything goes incredibly fast. The buyers sign the contract, the funds are wired, the deed is transferred, and by some stroke of miracle, Mathieu has pushed enough people to get this taken care of in a single day, something completely unheard of in the real estate industry.

When she hands him the keys to his brand-new Tuscan cottage in the outskirts of Paris, she just assumes that their date is canceled. She secretly hopes that at least they can postpone it.

"So, I guess that is everything," Violette says, not sure what kind of response awaits her.

"What are you talking about? You owe me a date. We have two things to celebrate. One, the house. And two, the fact that you agreed to go on a date with me."

"We can do this some other time." She really doesn't want to feel like an obligation.

"Are you bailing on me?"

"No, I just thought that you might want to move a few things in and get settled. It's a big day."

"Violette," he says taking her hand, "I want to celebrate all of this with you. Give me two hours. Instead of me picking you up, would you mind coming over? I'll call you a taxi. That is the only change of plans I see."

"Okay."

"You mean it?"

"Yes," she says, "and I'll drive myself."

He squeezes her hand. "All right, I will see you in a little while!"

Violette stops by the hospice to squeeze in a quick visit with her mom and then goes home to take a shower and change clothes. She has absolutely no idea what this date with Mathieu will be like, but she is so looking forward to spending an evening with him without the added duty of being his realtor. Tonight, her fairy godmother is breaking her dateless cycle, and Violette's heart flutters with anticipation and nerves.

She makes the trek over to Mathieu's new house and knocks on his door right on time. He opens it, and she gasps when she sees how he has transformed the living room. Everywhere she looks, there are candles. Dozens and dozens of small white tea candles illuminating the room and romanticizing the moment. She can't believe someone has gone to all of this trouble for her, especially on a first date.

Sitting in the middle of the canopy of candles is a picnic blanket with the most scrumptious-looking spread that Violette has ever seen. She has no idea what to say, so she just stands there in the doorway with her mouth gaping.

Mathieu has an irresistible grin on his face, and he watches her expression. "What do you think?"

"What do I think? Oh, Mathieu, this is wonderful. Not bad for a first date."

"Well, come in. Come sit next to me." He pours her a glass of red wine in a stemless goblet.

She obliges without hesitation and takes the wine glass. Without even taking the first sip, she is so happy she feels drunk, not believing that this is her real life. She takes a sniff of the wine, its sweet aroma filling her nostrils, and takes a sip, a tiny bit just for taste. She revels in its deep ruby flavor and acidic structure.

"Do you like it?" Mathieu asks, watching her.

"It's good, but I can't believe you did all of this for me."

"The wine is a Cabernet Sauvignon. My brother, Alain, is an anthropologist, and he travels all over the place. He brought this back from Egypt as a Christmas present. And Violette," he says, pausing after her name, "I would do anything for you."

The sense of sincerity in his voice makes her melt. If she were a slice of butter, she would be sizzling on fire in a hot skillet. She looks down at her wine and takes another sip, so unused to the compliments and flattery.

"Look at me," he says with authority.

Once again, she obliges.

"I think you are beautiful, Violette Deschamps."

She blushes. Trying to be more confident, she returns a shy smile back to him. He pours himself a glass of wine. He joins her on the picnic blanket and sits close, very close, to Violette.

She changes the subject away from her. "Your brothers and sisters, you all lead such interesting lives. Anthropologists, movie directors, you in the music industry."

She knows he works in the music industry, just not the full capacity.

"Our parents taught us never to settle. So we don't. If you could do anything, what would it be?"

"Interior design."

"That was a quick answer. Why don't you?"

"I went to school for it, but then I had to stop classes. Real estate was the closest thing."

"It's not too late to go back, make your dream a reality."

"Maybe one day."

"In the meantime, you are the cutest, sweetest realtor I have ever known. Just don't flirt with all your hunky single clients."

She laughs. "Only you! You are a devious one, Mr. Deneuve."

"Are you hungry?"

"I'm starving, actually. Now that I think about it, I hardly had time to eat anything."

He takes his hand and gently touches her chin.

"Well, let's change that, shall we?"

"Mathieu, you have enough food to feed a dinner party for a small country!"

"I wasn't sure what you liked, so I got a little bit of everything."

They start off with a main course of fish with a divine garlic and lemon sauce. Violette loves how comfortable their banter is. They flip-flop between serious conversations about growing up and dreams and traveling and flirtatious comments.

"This fish is heavenly."

"So are you, Violette."

"You are laying it on thick. You know I'm already here, right?"

"I can't help it! I want you to feel special."

"Mission accomplished."

After their fish, the next course is a simple salad with a balsamic dressing.

"So, how do you like your place?" Violette asks him as she pushes the tomatoes on the salad to the side of the bowl.

"Oh man, it's incredible. I love it. I can't wait to move in fully and make this my home. There is just one thing that I need."

"What's that?"

"I need to find a good decorator," he says with a sly look. "Do you have any recommendations?"

"There are two that I usually recommend."

"Seriously, Violette, your name better be one of them."

"Oh, I don't know. I couldn't."

"Confidence, Violette! You need to be more confident. I insist that you help me. It will be so much fun. I won't take no for an answer."

She says okay, trying to suppress a squeal of glee that she feels inside.

Then Mathieu presents Violette with a cheese plate, and the conversation flows easily between the two.

"Can I tell you a secret?" she says.

"Violette Deschamps has a secret? I'm intrigued!" He sits up straighter, curiosity piqued.

"This is my dream house. I swear I literally saw this place in my sleep."

"It's fate then. You, me, the house. For tonight, it's fate."

He grabs the desserts, dark chocolate crème brûlée garnished with raspberries.

They munch and talk and munch and talk, and a few hours race by without either of them realizing it. Violette sees what time it is and knows that she should be getting back.

"This has been fun, Mathieu. Thank you. I mean it, this was a really special night."

"You know, Violette, you don't have to leave. Stay with me. Please? It'll be fun!"

She laughs, thinking that he is joking.

"No, I'm serious. Stay with me. Please, please, please?"

She looks at him incredulously.

"For one week," he demands.

"A week? You are crazy!"

"You can help me decorate, and this wonderful date won't have to end."

He looks so hopeful, and if Violette is being honest, she doesn't want to go home to an empty apartment. Yet, she tends to be cautious, never fully jumping into anything without careful consideration.

"Give me one night to think about it. It's been a crazy day, and I'm exhausted. Besides, I don't even have a toothbrush here."

"So you'll say yes tomorrow?"

"I'm saying we will see."

"But it's not a no?"

"It's not a no, Mathieu."

"I guess this is good night then."

There is an awkward pause that happens at the end of every first date. Hug, kiss, shake hands, or none of the above?

Mathieu reaches out and grabs Violette's hand, softly and gently, before taking a step closer to her.

"I wish you would stay."

She looks up at him with innocent eyes. He stands a full head taller than she does, and he takes another step closer. He cups her chin with his right hand, his left hand still interlocked with the hands of the woman he deeply cares about.

"Violette Deschamps, may I kiss you?" he asks, and she detects nerves in his voice, which she finds unexpected. She nods her head to indicate yes.

He tilts her head up and leans down to give her a soft, sweet good-night kiss. It isn't long, but they both think that it's a perfect ending to a perfect date.

"Good night, Violette."

"Good night, Mathieu."

CHAPTER TWENTY

Mathieu Deneuve closes the door, blows out the candles, and goes to sleep in his new home with an uncontainable giant grin on his face.

He knows what he has with Violette is the start of something special.

In the morning, Violette wakes up, and for a moment she can't figure out if last night really happened or if it was all a dream.

When she looks at her phone, she sees she has a new message from Mathieu. It simply reads, *Say yes! One week!*

If she is honest with herself, she can easily take a week off of work. She has never taken more than a day or two off in a row, and with the massive sale of the Tuscan cottage, she is a hero around the office. Even though it is a Sunday, she heads into the office to finalize the paperwork for her closing with Cynthia DeFleurs and calls Jean-Philippe.

"Violette, what are you doing at the office on a Sunday?"

"I'm finishing up some paperwork, and I'm calling to ask a favor."

"Sure. What is it?"

"Can you cover my meeting with Cynthia and let me have the week off?"

There is a pause on the other end of the line.

"Is everything okay?"

"Actually, everything is more than okay. I just wanted to take a personal week off. If that's okay."

"I think that sounds great. I am so happy to see you taking care of you. It's about time. Leave the paperwork on Brigitte's desk, and I'll see you in a week!"

"Thanks, Jean-Philippe."

Having that taken care of, Violette goes to visit her mom.

Upon getting to the hospice center, she learns that her mother has developed a touch of pneumonia, which is always worrisome, but especially so to a woman in Lydia's frail state.

She does her normal routine with her mom, including curling her hair this time. She tells her mom all about her date and Mathieu's crazy proposal to spend seven days together. Her mother coughs several breathy, raspy coughs, and it breaks Violette's heart to leave. She promises to come see her mom again soon.

When she gets to the front desk, Nadine is there, thank goodness.

"Hey, Nadine, I'm going to be absent from my visits the next week."

"What kind of plans do you have going on, girl?"

"A minivacation with a friend."

"Well, it's about dang time! Good for you."

"Since I'll be gone, could you do me a favor and do my nighttime routine with Mom? I wrote down on the card what to do. You can do it or the other night nurses can do it, but I would really appreciate it. I'll have my phone with me if you need anything."

"We will take the best care of Miss Lydia for you. Don't worry, just have fun, and take care of yourself."

"Thanks, Nadine."

Feeling relieved, Violette gets into her car. Before she drives away, she takes a deep breath. Is she really going to do this? Spend an entire week with Mathieu?

When her car pulls into the long driveway leading to his house, he greets her before she has even stopped.

He runs out the door. When she steps out of the car, he picks her up, embraces her in a hug, and twirls her around.

"Does this mean you're staying? Is this a yes?"

"This is what yes looks like," she says with a smile.

Neither one of them have any idea what this week will hold. They are unsure of this new relationship, if it can even be called that yet this early on. But in this moment, there is a mutual feeling of hope floating through the air, radiating the bubble they will share the next seven days, the next one hundred and sixty-eight hours.

Mathieu carries Violette's bag into the house. He made a trip to his flat in Paris earlier in the day, so there are a few essentials in the home, but still no furniture, not even chairs to sit in. There are however, a plethora of blankets and pillows.

"I thought we could just camp out until I get more stuff here. I actually want to see what my decorator thinks. I'm thinking I might need to get new furniture, start from scratch." He winks at her. "That is a project for tomorrow. Tonight, we pick up right where we left off."

He wraps her in his arms and gently kisses her, and she can sense urgency, passion in his touch. She gives in to the kiss and slowly wraps her arms around his neck. She finally takes a step back, and he releases his hug on her. He knows Violette is the type of girl who takes things slow, and he is perfectly okay with that.

Not wanting to pressure her or make her uncomfortable, he changes the subject.

"I brought board games back! I had a feeling you would stay, and I thought we could play. These are some of my favorites, and they are good, clean, wholesome, old-fashioned fun," he says earnestly. "But I have to warn you, I am quite competitive."

The first game, Violette wins.

"I guess I'm pretty competitive too, eh?"

"I let you win that round. I'm convinced you cheated!" he jokes.

"I think the winner should get a kiss," Violette says.

"Then losing is my new favorite thing," he retorts as he leans in for another kiss.

They play a few more rounds, and then Mathieu announces that he is ready for dinner.

He makes a frozen pizza in the oven, and they both think it tastes wonderful, although neither of them care one bit about the food. It is impossible to when the company is so sweet.

"I don't have cable yet, but I thought we could watch a movie or something. I hooked the DVD player up, and I have a handful of movies to choose from. Anything you want."

She looks through the DVDs. Mathieu loves just watching her. Being picky has never looked so perfect.

"Sorry I don't have any couches or anything. Blankets and pillows and a living room campout will have to work."

"Works for me," Violette says as she puts the DVD in the player and presses the power button to turn on the television.

The movie starts to play. About five minutes in, Violette looks at him. "You are watching me, not the movie." She playfully shoves him.

"You are much more interesting than this movie."

"It's your movie!"

"But I like you more."

She rolls her eyes, and he scoots closer to her on the blanket and wraps his arm around her.

Violette feels as though she is a teenager in high school again, flirting, hand holding, and stealing little kisses in the boring parts of the movie. The movie might be playing as background noise, but for tonight, Violette and Mathieu only care about the scenes from their budding romance.

As the credits to the movie flash on screen, Violette giggles. "I barely know what happened in the movie."

"You didn't miss much."

"You kept distracting me!"

"You get distracted easily then."

"Mathieu, seriously?" she says, stifling a yawn.

"You can't be tired already!"

"I'm not!" she says while trying to fight back another yawn.

"Liar," he says, kissing her on the forehead. "But you are the cutest liar I know."

She leans into him, and he can feel the goose bumps on her arm.

"You're cold," he states.

"I guess I am a little bit cold," she admits, leaning into his chest.

"I know it's getting late, but I am wide awake. Let's start a fire in the fireplace. I'll stay awake until the embers go out. You can sleep."

"That's creepy. You're just going to watch me sleep?" she says, raising a skeptical eyebrow.

"Not like that, you weirdo!" This time, he rolls his eyes at her.

He stands up and goes outside to get the firewood. He's only gone for less than a minute, but when he comes back, Violette is curled up on the sea of blankets and pillows.

"Violette?"

When he gets no response, he walks over and sees that her eyes are closed and she is sleeping.

He can't help but smile at her sweetness. He puts the logs on the fire, and it starts to crackle. She wakes up.

"Shhhh," he whispers. "Go back to sleep."

She nods her head yes and leans back into him.

"This is kind of an awkward question, but, Vi, do you want to, er, sleep in different rooms? We can separate the blankets out if you want."

She puts a finger up to her mouth indicating for him to be quiet.

"Just sleep?" she asks, although this is more of a demand than a question.

"Just sleep."

She snuggles into his arms, and almost instantly she falls asleep.

As she sleeps, Mathieu soaks in the warm glow from the fire and the one growing in his heart. Once the embers turn from orange to black, Mathieu kisses Violette on the cheek, tucks her in, and falls asleep right beside her.

CHAPTER TWENTY-ONE

The next morning, Violette wakes up first and feels more refreshed than she has in a long time. Normally, she never sleeps well the first night in a new place, but with Mathieu right beside her, she feels right at home.

She can't believe that she is with Mathieu in this house of her dreams.

Since Mathieu is still sleeping, she tiptoes out of their fort of blankets and pillows and makes an entrance into the kitchen, hoping to find enough ingredients to surprise her man with breakfast. She assumes that since he made dinner for her two nights in a row, that his fridge is fully stocked.

She was wrong.

The takeout bag is peeking out of the garbage can, and she sees the receipt from Chez Louis. He didn't skimp on anything, and he paid a price for it. There is nothing suitable for breakfast, lunch, dinner, or a snack. She can't even brew tea. Surprisingly, there is tea, but no pot or kettle to boil water.

She pulls out her phone and starts typing up a list of things Mathieu needs... just in case he needs a little extra help. Giving up on the pursuit of breakfast, she heads back into the living room where Mathieu is still sleeping. She crawls back under the covers, trying to be ever so quiet so that he can stay asleep. Her best attempt isn't good enough, because he opens one eye.

"Good morning, beautiful," he says, half asleep still.

"Good morning to you!"

He rolls over on his side to face her. "You are way too chipper in the morning. Mornings are for sleep," he says, half joking, half serious.

"I'm used to it. But go back to sleep."

"I don't want to waste a single second of these seven days."

"Go back to sleep, Romeo!"

He listens. And Violette doesn't mind the quiet, the peace of her dream home with her dream man. All of this is surreal, she tells herself, soaking in each second that passes like a sponge. These are the type of memories people remember fifty years from now, the type of memories that even if the outcome is less than desired, the regret is never there. Violette doesn't take a single moment of this for granted.

While he sleeps, she starts getting ready for the day. She takes a shower, brushes her teeth, and puts on her makeup. When she goes back downstairs, Mathieu is finally awake.

"Good morning again," Mathieu says.

"Again?" Violette says. "Yep, we had this same conversation earlier, but I'm pretty sure you were talking in your sleep."

"Ha, I have no recollection of that. Anyway, how'd you sleep?"

"Good."

"Do you always wake up looking this pretty?"

"Always," Violette says with a wink.

"So what do you want to do today? We can do anything your sweet little self wants."

"I think you need to go shopping. Groceries, those newfangled things called pots and pans.

And do you know how hard it is to shower without towels?"

"Nope, but I like to picture it," he says mischievously.

Violette blushes and ignores his crude comment.

"Okay, you're right. I do need some basics for my bachelor pad. You can have free rein over what I get."

"No, no, no! I'll help, but this is your place. I don't even know how often you cook or what you have at your apartment."

"I'm just going to start fresh. I'm not sure my stuff will fit into my new cottage villa."

"What are you going to do with your old stuff?"

"Just throw it away probably."

"Will you at least donate it to shelters or churches?"

"My little Violette Deschamps, the saint. You are such a better person than I am. For you, yes."

"You are crazy."

"You keep saying that, but I know," he says, wrapping her in a big hug. "I'm never letting go."

Violette hopes this is true.

Later that afternoon, the new couple shops in town. Mathieu tries to conceal his identity. Fortunately, the sun is out, so sunglasses and a baseball hat help with that.

"I really am terrible at home décor," Mathieu says. "Whatever you want to do with the place is fine with me. I trust you completely."

"This is going to be fun!" She walks through the door of a decor shop that Mathieu is holding for her.

"First up, I made a list of essentials that you need. Let's start with the kitchen. You don't cook much, do you?"

She stops at the pots and pans section.

"I made dinner last night."

"No, you're a liar. I saw the takeout bag in the trash and the frozen pizza. Come on!"

"You snoop!"

Violette laughs and puts a couple of basic pots and a frying pan in the cart.

"But I can cook. I make a wickedly delicious marinara sauce. And that pizza was baked to perfection. I should get an award. Best frozen pizza chef ever."

"You'll have to make the marinara sauce for me," she says, wheeling the cart to the towels.

As they shop, they talk about music. Mathieu is floored that Violette isn't into the entertainment industry, rarely watches TV and movies, and doesn't follow the music scene. She's just so refreshing.

They talk about art and paintings that they've seen at the Louvre. Even though it's filled with tourists, they both love it. They talk about some of the lesser known galleries in Paris, comparing which one they've been to and which ones they still need to visit.

As Violette chooses several neutral-toned colors of towels and a white linen shower curtain and puts them in the cart, they talk more about his family. The Deneuve family has some good stories, and she finds herself longing to meet them. The more she knows about his family, the more she fantasizes about what it would be like to be Mrs. Violette Deschamps Deneuve.

Violette Deneuve.

It sounds good together, she thinks, her lips curving into a slight smile.

"What are you thinking about?" he asks as they walk in tandem through the aisles.

"Nothing."

She would never admit this to him, especially because she feels like this whole crazy scenario feels too good to be real. It's too perfect, and she wants to guard her heart, even though some heartbreaks are worth the risk.

They stop to pick up some groceries and laugh at each other's selections, marveling at how very different they are from another.

They get back just in time to meet the man who is setting up the Internet. While the man hooks up the wireless routers, and installs the proper cables, Mathieu and Violette make sandwiches and sit on the back patio.

They eat in a comfortable silence, and then out of nowhere, Mathieu asks, "So what would you do if you had your own interior design business?"

Violette doesn't even hesitate to think about it. "I would help clients create their perfect, dreamlike oasis. Oh, and for clients on a budget, help them thrift shop and create million-dol-lar-looking pieces for mere euros with time and effort. I love DIY projects! Turning something old into something new—it's my passion."

Mathieu notices she gets a spark in her eye when she talks about all of this.

"So do it!"

"One day, I hope to."

"You can use my home as a portfolio builder. I think you should go for it."

"I can't just stop working as a realtor without having something more solid."

"Well, start small. You picked out items that are perfect for me. And I'm not an easy guy to please."

Violette laughs and takes a bite of her sandwich. "That's true."

"I believe in you," he says.

She can tell that he means it.

The Internet guy comes outside to let them know that everything is hooked up.

"Perfect timing. Let's start on that portfolio of yours. Want to pick out my furniture?"

"I do!"

They go inside, and Mathieu grabs his laptop.

Violette pulls up a few of her favorite furniture stores' websites, and Mathieu watches as Violette expertly puts couches and chairs of different shapes and fabrics together.

"I love all of these. I really do, Violette."

"Choose one."

"Okay, I like option number three."

She thought he would like that one best, with the oversized deep-chocolate brown leather sectional and double ottoman with a lighter brown and tan fabric. For details, she adds a tray to sit on the ottoman, several funky cream-colored vases to sit on the fireplace mantle, and an array of brown, tan, and off-white throw pillows.

"Click the rush order option. I want to get this as quickly as possible."

She does as he says, although her eyes bulge out at the price of everything. He pulls out his credit card and doesn't even bat an eye as he types in his number and security code.

"I love this, Violette!" He kisses her once on the lips, draws back, and then kisses her again for a long time. When they finally pull apart, they both feel dizzy.

"I'll be right back," he says and dashes up the stairs. Upon his return, he brings his guitar with him and tells her that he wrote a song for her.

"You wrote a song for me?"

Mathieu loves the innocent look she gives him.

"I did. I told you, you are my muse. My totally cute and kissable muse."

Before she can say anything, he starts strumming on his guitar and belts out a song that touches Violette to the core. It's full of feelings and happiness and emotion. More than anything, it represents how he feels about her, and she is stunned in the best possible way.

***

Over in Paris, one very frustrated Xavier Deneuve calls Madeleine. He is surprised she picks up.

"I can't find him anywhere."

He tells her about the real estate agency lead.

"Go back and use my name."

"They already know I'm your brother."

"Tell them it's a giant favor to me. Or better yet, I'll send Jean-Philippe an e-mail. Something really weird is going on. You know Mathieu, there is no telling what goes on in his mind."

"Sounds good, Madeleine. Update me when you get some news."

Right after the phone call, Madeleine flips through her contacts and finds Jean-Philippe's e-mail. She types:

Jean-Philippe!

I miss you and everyone at Domaines D'Elegance. We are having a family emergency and are trying to find our brother Mathieu. We think he gave you an alias. Could you please help us out? Have you seen him? It's important. I wouldn't ask unless it was critical. I'm out of the country. Please work with Xavier, my other brother. He stopped in earlier.

Thanks,

Madeline Deneuve

Since Jean-Philippe is always working, he sends back a reply almost instantly requesting Xavier to stop by. Madeleine calls Xavier and lets him know.

Two hours later, Xavier is back at the Domaines D'Elegance office.

Jean-Philippe knows exactly who Xavier is now and is much friendlier toward him today.

"It's against our policy and protocol to reveal client information. However, I don't know what is going on and what the emergency is. I am going to breach the normal procedure. I can tell you that Mathieu did buy a property with us. He closed just a few days ago. I went through his realtor's files, and he had to use his legal name on all of the closing documents."

He hands Xavier a piece of paper with Mathieu's address.

"Thank you, sir. Thank you so much!" Xavier takes the piece of paper and sets off to find Mathieu.

CHAPTER TWENTY-TWO

*A*drien Henri is in his Parisian office and has spent the past week sifting through the video audition submissions. He has literally done nothing but eat, sleep, and watch videos. Some of them have been excruciating, but he knows this is the best way to exert power over Les Slinks and keep his promise to the guys.

He is nearing the end of his "six weeks, tops" declaration, and he has found "the one."

This guy is Mathieu version 2.0. He knew it as soon as he hit play on this singer's video. Within five seconds, he clapped his hands together and squealed like the little pig that he is.

His name is Vincent Yves, and Adrien loves him. He's a younger singer, which means he will be easy to manipulate. Plus, Vincent has so much potential. That is evident from his stage presence and both his singing and guitar-playing abilities.

It's *a dream come true*, Adrien thinks, and he paces in his office, stretching from his long stints of sitting at his computer. He has no intentions of watching any more of those darn submission videos.

Adrien throws his hands in the air. Aloud, he says, "Is Vincent Yves really the right guy? Don't blow this, Adrien."

He comes to the conclusion that he honestly has no idea, but time is running out. He has to bring a leading man to Les Slinks, and Adrien does what Adrien says he will do. He knows his motives can be questionable, but no one can claim that he breaks promises. And this is one promise that benefits him. If there's no Les Slinks, there is no fancy house by the Mediterranean.

His mind wanders back to Vincent Yves. Vincent has the same build as Mathieu, wears similar clothes as Mathieu does, and has the same hair color as Mathieu. His face is memorable, the kind of kissable face that will make the girls go wild. His voice, well—eh, it's forgettable. With the catchy songs that make people want to turn the radio up, roll the windows down, and let their hair blow in the wind, anybody with a decent face will work. Vincent it is!

Adrien sits down at his desk and starts drawing up some plans, his success kit for Les Slinks. There are hundreds and thousands of bands and singers in this world, maybe millions including all the unknown groups. The difference between the unknowns and the well-known is that one has a recording label and the other does not.

"All I need to do is work my business magic. It's a numbers game." He says this to the wall. He pulls up the contact information provided with Vincent's video submission and gives him a call.

It rings.

It rings again.

And Adrien hears a voice. "Vincent Yves."

"Hello, Vincent? My name is Adrien Henri. I am the record executive for the band Les Slinks. I received your video submission, and out of the thousands we went through, we want you!"

The thousands of videos bit may have been a slight exaggeration, but hey, who is counting?

"No way. That's totally rad! Count me in. Do I need to come meet the band and play with them? This is awesome, dude!"

Adrien wishes he did not sound quite as eager. Dare he say that he misses Mathieu's brooding artist self? It worked for their image. This guy sounds too peppy, but what can he do? He sighs quietly.

"Yes, that is exactly what we are going to do. Welcome to Les Slinks!"

Adrien and Vincent set up a meeting, and as soon as he gets off the phone, he gives Guillaume, Marcel, and Olivier a call for an emergency meeting the next day. He doesn't tell them the reason, but only that he has good news.

***

The next day, the four of them are crammed into the tiny, trendy office.

"Any luck with the Mathieu manhunt?" Adrien asks, trying to show that he is an ally of the band.

"Nothing but dead ends. It sucks. It really sucks," Marcel says.

"Yeah, I was hoping you were going to give us a box and surprise—Mathieu jumps out!" Olivier says.

"Well, my news is good for the band, but unfortunately, it is not Mathieu. However, it's better than Mathieu! May I present to you, Mathieu Deneuve version 2.0. Dun, dun-a, dah!"

He tries to make the first glimpse of their new lead singer dramatic by dimming the lights and hitting the play button to Vincent Yves's video.

"This," he says, pointing to the screen with his short, chubby fingers, "is Vincent Yves. I present to you the new lead singer of the new and improved Les Slinks!"

When the video stops, Adrien looks as though he is awaiting a standing ovation. Instead, he gets blank stares from the band. Clearly, this isn't the reaction that he was hoping for.

"Who are the other choices?" Guillaume asks.

"What other choices?" Adrien responds.

"You said you would present several choices and we got the final word," Marcel says.

"Yeah, you promised," Olivier chimes in.

"There was no comparison." Adrien is getting defensive now.

He sighs in frustration, wondering if an all-female band would be easier to manage than these depressed, questioning musicians. He walks over to his laptop computer on his desk.

"Fine, you are right. I did promise to let you choose from the top contenders. Let me pull up a few other examples."

He turns off the projector screen so that the guys can't see that he is moving the mouse to the file titled "Worst Auditions" and chooses two at random. He presents them to the band.

They watch the first audition, and it is so bad that everyone in that room, including Adrien, feels as if they are watching a brutal horror movie scene. The second is only slightly better, although that is still not a compliment to the artist by any means.

"Seriously? These are awful. Where did you find them?" Marcel asks.

"Does it matter? We have our guy. Give him a chance, will you?"

"I still say we give Mathieu a few more days. At least let the crazy guy have his two months of being in Mathieu-land," Olivier says.

"Time is up, the ship leaving Mathieu-land has sailed home, and unfortunately, he wasn't on the boat. The studio dates are already scheduled for a month out, and we are working nights and days until this release is perfect. Do

I make myself clear? You know how hard it is to get in with this studio. We can't push it back. Who knows how long it will be until their next opening." Adrien starts pulling their contract back out for what feels like the umpteenth time, and his face is flushed with frustration.

"Put the contract away, Adrien." Marcel waves the contract away with his hand. "Give us a minute?"

Adrien nods his head and steps out of the conference room to give Les Slinks some privacy.

"What do you think? Should we give this Vincent Yves guy a try?" Marcel asks.

"I say we don't have a choice," Olivier says.

"I'm in. And truthfully, he's not bad. He has potential." Guillaume looks down at his feet upon admitting this.

"He is not Mathieu though," Olivier retorts to Guillaume.

"Okay, okay, let's not go down that road. If Mathieu comes back, then what?" Marcel questions with a look of defeat spreading on his face.

"Then we can reevaluate," Olivier says. "It's our band."

"All right, so this is a band agreement? We are all okay with giving Adrien's plan a try? Everyone sitting in this room is a hundred percent on board?"

"Yeah, I guess so, Marcel. Although, I never thought Adrien would ever have this much power over us. It really sucks. This whole situation! I hate Mathieu right now." Guillaume leans back in his chair.

"Don't say that." Olivier shoots Guillaume an unpleasant look.

Marcel ignores them both. "Me either. I never thought Adrien would be like this, but what choice do we have?"

Before anyone can answer that, Adrien waltzes back into the room.

"Well, what is the verdict?" Adrien scrunches up his face and scratches his chin.

"We are willing to meet with Vincent, but when Mathieu comes back, we have to reevaluate the situation."

"Wonderful! Now, in the meantime, I want you all to be working on new lyrics. Write songs all day, all night. This is going to be the best album yet, you wait and see!" Adrien says this hoping that he is right. This is a crapshoot even for him; however, he will do everything in his power to make sure that Mathieu Deneuve stays far away from any stage that Les Slinks steps foot on from here on out.

Once the band leaves for the day, Adrien writes a press release announcing that Les Slinks has a new lead singer. As he writes, he has a celebration for one. He opens the door to his minifridge that he keeps stocked in his office and carefully selects a bottle of champagne, a dry, aged bottle from Brittany. He grabs a champagne flute; he has two dozen in a cabinet, used for celebrating milestones with his bands and artists.

He pours the golden, fizzy liquid into his flute and takes a pack of cigarettes out of the breast pocket of his shirt and lights one, inhaling the scent of tobacco and sipping, well, chugging, glass after glass of champagne. He drinks, he smokes, and he writes the headline of his news release: Les Slinks Replace Lead Singer Mathieu Deneuve.

CHAPTER TWENTY-THREE

*B*am! *Bam! Bam! Bam! Bam!*

"What in the heck was that?" Violette looks around, surprised by the sound of knocking. It sounds like an angry, rabid woodpecker on steroids.

Bam! Bam! Bam! Bam! Bam!

"I think someone is at the door. Stay here."

Bam! Bam! Bam! Bam! Bam!

The knocking becomes louder and more forceful.

Secluded from other houses, they have no idea who or what it might be. Mathieu opens the door, and a look of complete shock clouds his expression.

"Xavier? What? How did you find me? What you are doing here?"

"Surprise!" Xavier throws his hands in the air as if he were on a roller coaster. He stands on the front porch, putting his hands in his back pockets. He looks relieved, but not exactly thrilled to see his older brother. They stand there, staring, neither sure what to say. Xavier cracks the silence like ice skates on a frozen pond.

"Mathieu, we need to talk."

"Come on in. Is everything okay?" He opens the door wider and waves Xavier inside, fearing something awful has happened. Was it with his mom? Dad? Is someone sick? His first instinct is that someone must have died. He cannot come up with any other reasons why Xavier would have tracked him down.

Violette walks out of the kitchen area where she had just finished washing and drying the new pots and pans. They still need to be put into the cupboards, but she peers around the doorway, curious to know what is going on. Xavier spots her.

"Seriously, Mathieu? You disappeared for a girl? I should have known." He shakes his head in utter disbelief.

Violette has a pained look on her face. This wasn't exactly how she wanted to meet Mathieu's family.

"It's not like that," Mathieu says, quietly.

Violette steps forward and shyly introduces herself to Xavier.

"I'm Violette Deschamps."

"Xavier," he says with a nod. "I'm sorry, I don't mean to be rude, but can I have a minute alone with my brother?"

"Whatever you need to say, you can say it front of Violette."

"No, it's okay, I'll give you two some space."

She nods to Mathieu and scurries back to the kitchen, wondering what is going on. It's not hard to find out since they are talking loudly. She tries not to eavesdrop, but she can't help it.

"Mathieu, this is serious."

"Calm down and tell me what is going on."

"The band is trying to replace you. Marcel contacted Madeleine out of desperation, and she begged me to come find you."

"Wait, what?" Mathieu talks several decibels higher when he hears the news. "They can't replace me."

"They can, and they are. Your record exec has been holding auditions, and you are on your way out. This is serious. You can't keep just screwing around with your life."

"Xavier, stop. They can't replace me."

"Listen to me, please, Mathieu. I know you're stubborn, but please, this is your one chance to fight back. You need to return to Paris as soon as possible and get this mess sorted out. I'm on your side, but don't mess this up."

"Okay, okay." Mathieu is starting to panic. For the first time in a long time, he craves alcohol. He feels the adrenaline start to rush through his veins.

"The girl?" Xavier questions.

"She isn't just some girl. When I went to buy a house, she was my realtor, and this just sort of happened. I'll explain it all later."

"She's cute, but you cannot throw your entire career away like garbage. Don't put your emotions in one place. Violette seems nice, I'll give you that."

"I think it's the real thing, Xavier. I'm not sure I want to go back."

"Don't be crazy. You have to at least find out what's going on. You'll never forgive yourself."

Xavier looks around. "I can't believe you bought this house."

"Me either, but, Xavier, let me take care of a few things. I'll be in Paris tonight."

Xavier stops, his eyes popping. "Wait, you bought a house on a whim. Violette, is she pregnant? Did you elope?"

"No to both. It's nothing like that, I told you." He remains unusually calm. "I'm not sure how you found me, but, just thank you."

"We're family, bro. If you want out, I don't care. I just want you to do this on your terms. No regrets."

Mathieu nods. After Xavier leaves, he closes the door and is irritated with everything going on. Violette is quietly standing by the door, and she can sense that Mathieu is upset.

"What's going on?" she says calmly, although she has a clear picture based on what she heard. It takes a whole lot to stun or surprise Violette, but that is exactly how she feels.

"Les Slinks is trying to kick me out because I took a two-month break. We had just finished touring, and I needed a break, an escape. It was late, I was in a bar, and I wrote a note saying that I would be back in two months. I went to Madeleine's house and decided to buy a house, met you, and here we are." He looks up at her. "Have you heard of Les Slinks?"

"Not the music, no."

This time it's Mathieu's turn to be surprised. "Well, I'm the lead singer."

"So I've heard." She crosses her arms.

"I needed a break. I wanted respite from the spotlight. Violette, don't be mad. I saw the Domaines D'Elegance card and gave your office a call. Brigitte said your schedule was free, and when she asked my name, I got nervous. Luc is my other brother. Madeleine is actually my twin. Please, Violette, I just didn't want everyone to know who I was. I wanted to be normal, average."

Violette softens. "Have you lied about anything else?"

"No, it's been me. Everything, all of it. You have seen the real Mathieu, minus the whole lead singer title."

She uncrosses her arms. "I've never known a rock star before."

With a pained smile plastered on his face, Mathieu says, "There is a first time for everything." He offers a sheepish shrug. "You really had no idea who I was?"

"I knew you were a musician, but I don't follow the wild lives of celebrities. I think they're fake."

"Sometimes we are. But not with this, Violette. Hear me when I say that I'm falling for you. I was instantly attracted to you from the first minute I met you in that awful, hideous suit, which I hope you have burned."

Violette ignores his jab. "So, what's going to happen? You need to go back to Paris."

She barely has time to process these new developments, but her heart hurts because she knows that their seven-day bubble has burst and she doesn't know what comes after that.

The softness that Mathieu displayed just moments ago disappears and is replaced once again with a rage that frightens Violette.

"I'm not going back! I'm staying here. I'm done with music. They can replace me. My bandmates are traitors. I'm staying. I want to stay right here with you!" He is practically yelling.

"Mathieu, calm down," Violette says, not liking this side of him. She can certainly understand his disappointment, but he seems to be going a little extreme in her opinion.

"Violette, I'm staying. I'm done. It's that simple."

"Just sit down, and let's talk about this."

He sits on the bare floor, as the furniture has yet to arrive. She sits beside him.

With tears in her eyes, Violette chokes them back and firmly says, "Mathieu, I think you need to go. I won't let you stay here. I'm going to leave this afternoon and go back to my flat. I won't be the reason that you leave and give up on Les Slinks."

Mathieu knows she is right, but he doesn't want to face the world again. He sits, head in his hands, an eerie, uncomfortable silence between them.

"Look at me, Mathieu. You told me to chase my dreams. I am telling you do to the same."

He looks at her. His eyes meeting hers cracks her heart. She wants him to stay; she wants to beg him to stay. She wishes for a moment that he wasn't famous. But he is, and she has to let him go, at least to Paris.

"Will you come with me?"

"No," she says firmly, a single tear falling down her cheek.

Then another.

And another.

She can't help it.

"Mathieu, I don't belong in your world."

"You don't even know Les Slinks. How do you know if you fit into my world or not?" he jokes and half smiles.

She forces one in return.

"I have my mom, my job, my life. I can't. Please don't ask me to."

Her heart breaks even more as she says this, knowing that it is the right thing to do.

"Violette, my sweet Violette." He wipes her tears away with his palm. "This isn't good-bye." He says this with uncertainty. "Besides, you're in charge of decorating my house, remember? You can't bail on me now. I'll tell you what. I'm going to leave you my key. You can come and go as you wish and you need." He stands up and grabs his key ring, sliding off the house key and pressing it into the palm of her hand.

"And here, let's do this." He rummages around until he finds his checkbook in a miscellaneous box. He writes her a check with more than enough money to decorate the house and more. He rips it out of the checkbook and hands the money over to her.

"Mathieu, this is more than I need to fix your house up." She refuses to take the check.

"Take it. Consider this an investment in your dream house."

She gives him an apathetic look. Knowing she will insist on not taking that much money, he adds, "Okay, consider this an investment in your interior design career. I am your first paying client, and you are officially open for business."

She takes the check, folds it in half, and slides it in her back pocket. "I would take payment in the form of kisses."

He takes her hands. "That can be arranged." He lowers his mouth and places it onto hers.

When they finally break away, he adds, "But don't do that to anyone else. Just me." He winks.

"Just you," she whispers and tries to choke back the tears that could fall. She is so worried that this is the end before they ever have a chance to truly get started. What should she expect? Simple, fairly plain Violette Deschamps on the arms of a hunky celebrity? It just isn't going to be her reality.

"This isn't good-bye, my sweet Violette. This is I'll see you later. After my trip to Paris, I'll call you."

She nods, just barely.

"Listen to me, beautiful. I want you in my life, I need you in my life. You are my muse, and you make my heart full. I—I really like you."

He knows the longer he stands here, the harder it will be to leave. He gives her one last swift kiss good-bye and doesn't look back as he leaves his new chalet. He flees into the late-afternoon sun, gunning for a showdown with Adrien Henri.

CHAPTER TWENTY-FOUR

*A*s he rides in the backseat of a taxi, Mathieu starts to realize the magnitude of this situation. He becomes angrier with each second that ticks by. How could Adrien do this? What about Marcel, Olivier, and Guillaume? How could they just go along with this?

Mathieu's mind, body, and soul crave a shot of whiskey, vodka, or tequila. He needs the calming effect of liquor running through his veins. He roughly punches his cell phone to dial Adrien Henri.

Adrien answers with a short, unfriendly hello.

In a low, growling roar, Mathieu says, "You and I are going to have a meeting in your office now."

"Nice to hear from you," Adrien retorts.

Mathieu is in such a rage that he cannot muster the strength to say another coherent word.

Mathieu counts to three, remembering something Violette told him. She counts whenever she feels nervous or when she has a case of insomnia. Maybe it will work for stress, he thinks, counting slowly. *Please work. Please work.* He wills it, although his anger is too strong.

Giving up, he hangs up and calls Marcel instead. It rings for what feels like eternity, and just as Mathieu is about to hang up, Marcel picks up.

"Hey, stranger," Marcel says.

"Marcel, what in the hell is going on? I'm on my way to have a meeting. Call an emergency band meeting stat. Meet me there at Adrien's office with Guillaume and Olivier!" He barely takes a breath as the words fly out of his mouth.

"Dude, you need to calm down."

"Calm down? Why should I calm down?"

"We'll talk during the meeting. Just relax, man. I'll call the others, and we'll meet you immediately."

They get off the phone, and Mathieu cannot do anything else besides sink back in the car and feel miserable about this. He asked for two months. In his mind, this was totally reasonable. Sure, he could have checked in, and maybe a small part of him regrets not doing that small act. But they should have had the decency to give him the full two months.

Mathieu takes loud, breathy sighs in the backseat, which only seems to make him more frustrated, with every sigh adding fuel to the fire.

By the time the driver drops Mathieu off, he is so unbearably livid that he hardly feels human.

As he rushes into the office building with a look of fury on his face, strangers on the sidewalk stop to watch him and exchange puzzles glances among one another. Mathieu is in his own world and pays them no attention.

He rushes past the secretary and doesn't stop moving until he storms into Adrien's office.

"Well, well, well, look who finally decided to reappear from hibernation."

Mathieu takes a seat, shoots a look of daggers at Adrien, and throws him a warning.

"Do not say another word until the rest of the band gets here."

"Or what?" Adrien laughs. "You're out, buddy boy."

"Shut up," Mathieu growls. His phone beeps, and he looks at it to see a text message from Violette.

Everything is going to be okay! He reads it, and only then does he try to relax. Violette would hate him if she saw him like this. What would Violette do? Not this, he thinks and tells himself not to say another word until the band gets here.

They finally arrive. It feels as if he has been waiting for hours, although he realizes it has been only ten minutes.

All three bandmates share concerned glances when they see Mathieu. Angry steam practically radiates from his ears.

Olivier is the first to speak. "Hey, bro! We missed you."

"Sounds like it," Mathieu says back in a frigid tone.

Marcel doesn't even try to play nicely. "Sounds like it? That's your response? I have looked everywhere for you. I broke into your apartment, man. I practically stalked your family to find you."

Feeling defensive now, Mathieu says, "Yeah, but I said I was going undercover for two months. Why couldn't you respect that? Two months. That's it. But no, I couldn't even have that. You guys are insufferable."

"We are the insufferable ones? Look around, Mathieu. I fought for you. I am the one who tried to say hey, let's give him the time, even though I think you have been selfish." Marcel is yelling now. He points to Guillaume and Olivier and adds, "Besides, the three of us are on your side. You should be dealing with Adrien. He's the one who found your replacement, Vincent Yves."

Guillaume, normally the quiet one, calls for a time-out. "Guys, we aren't going to get anywhere. You sound like a bunch of sorority girls fighting over something stupid. Stop."

Shocked by Guillaume's outburst, they are silenced.

Guillaume continues, "Just sit down, and let's talk this through. Mathieu, please understand we are on your side."

Adrien clears his throat. "And I'm on the side of the best interest of the band."

"Really?" Mathieu looks at him skeptically. "You just want to make as much money off of our success as you can. You only think of yourself."

"That is not true, my dear boy. I have worked my butt off for Les Slinks. I have made you who you are today."

"No dice." Mathieu calls it like he sees it. "Do you even remember what our original vision of the band was? You have taken us off that path. You have ruined us. You are the reason I wanted, no, *needed* a break from Les Slinks." He slams his hand down on the table.

Marcel and Olivier exchange glances and nod their heads slightly in agreement with Mathieu.

"The crazy guy has a point, Adrien," Olivier chimes in. "Les Slinks was born to touch the hearts and souls of our listeners with poignant, emotive tunes. We tackle real-life issues. The songs are supposed to have soul to them."

"Yeah, not this poppy, formulaic everyday garbage that you want us to sing," Mathieu adds. "It's not us."

Adrien, who has kept trying to interrupt them, finally gets a word in. "It's that—and I quote—poppy, formulaic everyday garbage that has your music rising in the charts and the reason your venues are selling out."

"It's not, Adrien. Our music, minus your crap, is what gets the crowd going. I want for Les Slinks to get back to its roots."

"It's not your choice anymore, Mathieu." Adrien stops to laugh and shake his head. "You aren't even a member of Les Slinks. Mathieu Deneuve 2.0, also known as Vincent Yves, is going to replace you. Out with the old, in with new."

Marcel interjects, "Mathieu is right." Turning to his friend, he adds, "I'm angry with you, dude, don't get me wrong, but you are right. We have become another cookie-cutter, main-stream band."

Playing off of his hype, Mathieu looks Olivier and Guillaume in the eye. "So what do you say, guys? Are we done being Adrien's poppy puppets? Do you want to be led by men in suits, or do you want to be real artists again?"

"Artists," they both say, and Mathieu nods his head firmly with great satisfaction.

"And you are artists." They watch as Adrien's face turns red and he starts looking nervous. "However, you signed a contract and—"

"Enough with the darn contract already," Olivier says then turns to Mathieu. "He has done nothing but talk about this stupid contract."

"It's legally binding and would uphold in any court of law."

"I think you are forgetting one little piece of important information. We may have signed on with you, but we can break the contract as long as the four of us are in total, unanimous opinion. Our band, our rules! This guy," Mathieu says, pointing to Adrien, "this guy only wants to see how much money he can stuff in his pockets."

He turns back to his band mates. "Anyway, listen, bros, I am sorry. I am sorry that I disappeared and didn't keep you in the loop."

"Wait a second, we need to record this." Marcel takes out his phone and pulls up the video app. "Ladies and gentleman, Mathieu Deneuve is actually admitting he is wrong and he is apologizing? Who is this imposter, and what has he done with the real Mathieu Deneuve?"

"Very funny. Put it away," he says, smiling, starting to relax, albeit not much, but it's better than his irate state of mind.

Adrien gets awkwardly close to Mathieu to try to rejoin the conversation. "Well, I think we need to take a vote. I have already contacted Vincent, and we have a meeting scheduled. Do we want Vincent or Mathieu as the lead singer?"

"Really? A vote?" Marcel shakes his head.

"Yeah, really, Adrien?" Olivier says, exchanging a look with Guillaume, indicating that they think Adrien is being a total nimrod.

Mathieu, laughing at the ridiculousness of the situation, informs the group that he will be voting for himself.

"Mathieu!" the other three exclaim in unison.

"Well, hold on, now. My vote is for Vincent. I'm sorry, Mathieu, but you just are not responsible enough."

"Responsible enough? I said I would be gone for two months. I'm back right at the two-month mark. I'm not an accountant or a teacher or a lawyer. I'm an artist, and I like creative freedom. That means running Les Slinks the way that is conducive for our music. Had I followed your plan, I would have zero songs ready to record. Having my little escape and doing it my way, I have one killer song ready for recording. This is the real stuff, gentleman."

At Mathieu's outburst, Adrien seems speechless, a rarity for that man. He opens his mouth, but the words just don't come out, a gesture not lost by Mathieu. He continues, "And part of taking chances and taking a step backward, like my hibernation, yielded tremendous results. I've grown as an artist, and I think it's imperative that we take the next step as Les Slinks." He pauses and looks at Adrien. "This means, I think we need to find a new label. Clearly, Adrien isn't a good fit. He doesn't believe in me, therefore, he doesn't believe in us. It's a matter of simple philosophy."

Adrien sputters and turns red. "Now wait just a minute. According to our contract—"

"Dude, let it go. The contract is useless," Marcel quietly says.

"We missed you, man!" Olivier says to Mathieu, and Guillaume agrees by nodding his head.

Adrien once again tries to cut into the conversation, but Mathieu wastes no time in cutting him off. "So we are all in agreement. Adrien is out?"

Nods of agreement, except from Adrien, are shared. Guillaume puts his hand out, and the others lay their hands on top of Guillaume's, as if they were about to play a sports game. Olivier counts, "One, two, three," and they all chime in, "Les Slinks!" They raise their hands up and give high fives all around.

Adrien, now a few shades of red darker, finally interjects their celebrating. "We can work through this. We can make some changes. I want to represent Les Slinks. I think we just need to find a new balance and figure out how to get back on track. Remember, I made you the success you are today. I am the reason that you were able to tour as a headliner in the United States."

Mathieu steps closer to Adrien and stands much taller than he does. He looks down on Adrien as he speaks. "No, Adrien, our music did that. We were already filling up small venues before you came along. We need someone who understands our vision. That's not you."

"Well, this contract is legally binding, and it will uphold in court. We still have seven months with the current terms."

Mathieu pushes back the sleeve of his graphic T-shirt and reveals his muscular arms.

"Adrien, listen to us. We are done. I will pummel you if I need to."

"You wouldn't touch me."

"Wanna bet?" Mathieu steps closer and pulls back his arm as if he is ready to throw a punch. Adrien looks legitimately fearful.

Guillaume is the one who stops him. "It's not worth it, man. Let's get out of here."

Marcel steps in, agreeing with Guillaume. "Yeah, besides, we want to hear about this new song. And let's get started on the hunt for a new label!"

Olivier looks at Adrien in a peacemaking effort. "So what do you say, Adrien? Are you willing to part with us on civil terms? We appreciate what you have done for us, but I think we both admit that a separation will be mutually beneficial for both of us. No hard feelings?"

"Yeah, dude, we appreciate everything you have done for us. We don't want to stay enemies. The music industry is a small world."

Adrien sighs in resignation and knows that he is out. "I'm not sure how we went from kicking Mathieu out to kicking me out, but here is my verbal word that I am stepping down as Les Slinks' manager. I will draw up the official paperwork tomorrow."

The band is tactful enough to keep their celebrations to a minimum until they have left the office, but once they are outside, it's party time.

"So, Mathieu, we want to hear more about the new song."

"Yeah, and we want to know what you were up to the last two months."

"Was there a girl?"

"Oh yeah," Mathieu says. They walk into a nearby pub, and he relays the details–well, most of them–to his three best buds.

CHAPTER TWENTY-FIVE

*B*ack in her suburban flat, Violette's life has been totally flipped upside down, and she has Mathieu to thank. She hasn't seen him since he left for Paris that fateful afternoon, but he has inspired her to renovate her life.

She cried and cried after he called her to tell her that he left to record his album in Germany to work with a hot producer. She didn't realize that so many tears could fall from the eyes of any one human being. But in true Violette fashion, she picked up the broken pieces as if they were a shattered vase and slowly glued them back together, refashioning them into a new life for herself.

The next day, she typed her official resignation letter and walked into Jean-Philippe's office to tell him that she was quitting her job at Domaines D'Elegance. He was shocked, yet supportive, and they talked for a solid two hours.

She told him all about the Mathieu/Luc scandal, and she told him all about her dreams to open up her own interior design business. What she didn't expect was for Jean-Philippe to be so receptive. He made her a business offer she could not refuse. Domaines D'Elegance will recommend her to all their clients looking for interior designers. In return, the real estate agency will be given a ten percent referral commission. She is officially open for business, and she credits her fearlessness to Mathieu. She misses him fiercely, but her life is forever changed because of him.

They have shared a flurry of phone calls, Skype sessions, and love letters through e-mails, but he's been busy with the band, recording their new album independently—with the band's own money—and putting the plans to start his own label instead of signing another big recording contract.

Violette has had more than enough to keep her busy and her mind occupied. A couple of weeks after Mathieu returned to his real life, Violette received a phone call from Nadine.

When she picked up the phone, she knew the message waiting on the other end. Nadine tearfully informed her that her mother had passed away.

Violette swears that she knows when it happened. Lydia passed away in her sleep, and the night she passed, Violette woke up in the middle of the night with a wave of grief that overcame her. She once heard that when a loved one passes, someone very close, the living can actually feel the connection break when that person takes the last breath. That is exactly how she felt when she woke up and saw that the clock read 3:24 am.

Violette cried about that, again shocked by the amount of tears a single human could shed. Along with the grief, she experienced relief, an emotion that shocked her during this time. She knew the day was coming. She had tried to prepare herself mentally for the moment, but she still felt heartbreak. She didn't think her spirit could take much more dampening news.

On the other hand, Violette found great solace and relief in the fact that her mother was no longer sick, no longer suffering. Yet, she felt more alone than ever in this world. No parents, no family, no boyfriend or husband, and very few friends.

Violette arranged a small but beautiful service for her mother. Nadine and Jean-Philippe were by her side, and Mathieu sent a giant flower display that was stunning. Violette knows her mother would be pleased with how everything turned out. The skies were crystal-clear blue—there was not a cloud in the sky—and spring blossoms were blooming, awakening a new season of life.

She allowed herself three days to grieve and wallow. She watched TV and movies. She ate junk food. She cried. She slept, she napped, and she slept even more. On the third day, she pulled herself together. In her time of grief, she made great efforts to return to normal, although she had so much more free time now that she wasn't going to the hospice on a nightly basis. She wasn't sure how to fill those evening hours, and she missed Nadine's companionship.

Violette was also surprised by a hefty sum of money from her parents' life insurance policy. She wasn't expecting much, but thanks to her parents' careful planning, she had more than enough to live off comfortably for some time. She knew she would be getting some money, but to say that she was shocked would be an understatement. Shock seemed to be a common thread in Violette's life recently.

The extra cash gives her peace of mind as she starts this new adventure of starting her own business, although it's off to a booming start. For now, the decorating business is running from her home, but she hopes to find an office space soon, a place large enough where she can put together showrooms. Her dreams are big and she needs a big office to contain them.

Today, she sits at her desk with her laptop and attempts to get her website up and running. Her site is beautiful and classy, yet casual and down to earth. It represents Violette well. Her first big portfolio item is that of Mathieu Deneuve's house. It has brought a ton of hits to her site and has given her instant credibility. Not to mention, the work she did is beautiful–award-winning quality. Just as she promised Mathieu, she made his home impeccable. The furniture came, she organized it, and she carefully placed every last accent décor.

She laughs now at the memory of the large sectionals and heavy furniture she had to move by herself. When Mathieu asked about it, she told him that she didn't need help. She could do anything she set her mind to–and now she knows it's true. She sent Mathieu pictures, and she had a rush of adrenaline knowing that he loved it. It truly reflects what a spectacular home should be.

Anyway, she is sitting at her computer, working on the task, with the radio playing. Ever since Mathieu, she finds herself listening to music more and even reading the entertainment section of the newspaper, secretly hunting for any hints of what's going on with Les Slinks. What can she say? She's a silent fan girl.

She's just added a copyright statement to her website's footer when a song comes on the radio. It's a new song, one she has not heard before. The voice sounds familiar. When she turns up the volume, her heart starts racing.

It's the song that Mathieu wrote for her.

She closes her eyes and cherishes each second of the song, hearing Mathieu's voice, and hearing the words he wrote about her and their time together. She wants this moment to last, and when the song ends, too soon, in her opinion, she is smiling.

The radio announcer says, "Folks, that is Les Slinks with the first single off their new album. The band is actually in the studio with us this hour in honor of today's release. Again, that new album is called *Violette Nights*, and you can buy the eponymous single digitally today. Our next caller has a question for you, Mathieu Deneuve. Why don't you tell us—"

Violette doesn't waste a single second hearing what the disc jockey asks. On an impulse, she makes the spontaneous decision to rush over to the radio station. She knows it's crazy, but she drives as fast as she can. Traffic is not heavy, but she is shocked to find dozens upon dozens of fans outside the studio. Many of them have signs that say cutesy, catchy phrases, like "Marry me, Mathieu!" "I love Les Slinks," and "Les Slinks #1 Fan."

The radio station has a giant floor-to-ceiling window in the recording booth, so she can see Mathieu and the band along with the disc jockey, even from a distance. They also have a loud speaker system set up, so all the adoring fans can hear what's going on inside live. She can't find a parking spot, so she illegally parks on the sidewalk and rushes to the front of the crowd. She runs into some people and irritates a few others, but she doesn't care. She is so close to Mathieu, her Mathieu, yet he looks so different. She can tell he is in his element, and it makes her heart hurt. She feels like a silly child being here, but she can't pull her eyes away from him. She wants to turn around and go home, aborting her plan, but she is captivated by the love of her life just yards away.

The announcer says to the band, "All right, guys, why don't you give a wave to all your fans on the lawn!" She watches in slow motion as they turn and face the windows, waving like the famed celebrities that they are. They smile, they wave, and Mathieu stops. The announcer doesn't miss a beat.

"What do you see out there, Mathieu?" He pauses, and the band members exchange confused looks. Mathieu is frozen. The announcer makes a joke of some sort. He hears laughter around him, but none of it matters. He runs out the door.

The crowd buzzes with confusion and then excitement as Mathieu Deneuve rushes out the first-floor door and heads straight for them.

"Folks, we are not exactly sure what is going on. This is certainly unexpected." The announcer describes the scene to the audience over the live airwaves. "Mathieu Deneuve, here today with Les Slinks to celebrate the release of their new album, has just rushed into the crowd here at the studio."

Mathieu locks eyes with Violette and runs toward her, arms outstretched. Violette runs to him, and the crowd goes wild, most of the cheering, a few booing, when the two embrace. He lowers his head, and his lips touch Violette's lips. They share a long, passionate kiss. The world melts away around them. The crowd, the band, and the announcer watch as the scene unfolds.

"You're here," Mathieu says to her in between the kisses he can't stop giving her.

"I missed you."

Mathieu takes Violette's hand in his and raises them above his head as if they just won a gold medal in the Olympics. The crowd goes wild. Above the noise, the announcer asks the band, "What's going on? Who is this woman?"

Marcel informs him, the crowd, and the listeners on the radio, "This is the woman who inspired the album, Violette."

"What do you say? Let's bring her up and hear what the infamous Violette has to say. Folks, this is not planned. This will be new for all of us!" The announcer pumps up the crowd.

Olivier leans into the microphone. "Ladies and gentleman, let's give it up for Violette Deschamps!"

The crowd starts chanting her name. "Violette! Violette! Violette!"

Before Mathieu and Violette walk back upstairs to the recording booth, he dips Violette backward and gives her another kiss. Once again, the crowd goes wild.

Violette feels as if she is in a movie scene.

The two go back into the recording studio booth. The announcer is clearly thrilled that all of this is happening during his show. He capitalizes on the moment by asking, "All right, so I'm curious—and I know that a lot of listeners out there today are curious—Mathieu, does this mean you are off the market? No longer one of Paris's most eligible bachelors? What's the story? Give us the scoop!"

Mathieu laughs and shakes his head. Marcel leans into the microphone and speaks for him, knowing that Mathieu doesn't like to talk about his personal life. "Well, I guess the secret is out. Mathieu Deneuve is smitten with that pretty lady down there. Her name is Violette, as you all just heard. And now here we are, a true modern-day fairy tale."

Olivier takes a turn with the microphone. "So to answer your question, I'd say that for sure Mathieu is off the market. I've never seen him this happy before. We love the album, she's our muse, and we're glad she showed up today."

Mathieu and Violette sat down in front of microphones.

"I'm a big fan of grand gestures, and I haven't seen her in a couple of months," Mathieu says sheepishly, rubbing the back of his neck.

Shyly, Violette speaks into the microphone next, "Hi, everyone. Actually, this is a surprise for me too. I didn't know Mathieu named the album after me."

"Well, there you have it folks, I would say that Mathieu's leading lady has finally got the message! Thanks for tuning in. We'll play one more song from the new album, and we'll be talking more with Violette in a few moments."

CHAPTER TWENTY-SIX

*O*nce the radio show is finished, Violette is properly introduced to Marcel, Olivier, and Guillaume. They instantly love her.

"Do you have a sister?" Olivier flirts.

"If it's all right with you three," Mathieu says. "I'm going to take Violette to lunch. We have some catching up to do."

"I have a feeling we will be seeing a lot more of you," Marcel says with a head nod.

The boy say their goodbyes. Once the couple is alone in the hallway of the radio station, Mathieu kisses Violette once again. He breaks away only to say, "I can do this for the rest of my life."

Violette smiles. "So can I."

"Are you hungry?" he asks.

"A little bit. What about you?"

"Hungry for you," he says with a wink.

"You are so corny," she says, playfully rolling her eyes.

"Oh, you know you like it. You find me"—he pauses to kiss her—"irresistible!"

"That I do," she says, breathing in his masculine cologne and collapsing into his embrace.

"I was going to surprise you with the album when I got back in town, but you found me first."

He grabs her hand, and they walk into a nearby Greek restaurant. The restaurant is not crowded, but after they order, falafel pitas for them both, no tomatoes for Mathieu, the lovebirds settle into a corner booth. They sit on the same side of the table.

Not long after they cozy up in their booth, two pretty girls, a blonde and a brunette, approach their table. They're giggling, shy and nervous. The brunette nudges her friend to speak.

"You're Mathieu Deneuve of Les Slinks, right?" the blonde says to him.

He smiles back at them. "I am, indeed. What are your names?"

"I'm Hayley," the first girl says. She points at her friend. "And this is Laura. We're studying abroad in Paris this semester. We actually saw you open for the Strokes in New York. We've loved you since!"

"Well, thank you. I always love meeting fans."

"And is this Violette? We heard you on the radio today!" Laura, the brunette, exclaims.

"I am. It's nice to meet you two."

"We hate to bother you, but can we have your autograph?" Hayley asks.

The waitress brings out their food, and Mathieu pulls a pen out of his pocket. He grabs two paper napkins from the table and writes: *You can do anything. Enjoy Paris! Love, Mathieu Deneuve.* He hands each of the girls a napkin, although the message is hardly legible with his horrible handwriting.

The two students don't care one bit. Violette take pictures of the three of them with their cell phones.

Laura says, "Thanks so much. Enjoy your lunch!" The pair of friends walk away, squealing, and Mathieu fully expects to be tagged in their

Facebook, Instagram, and Twitter pictures later that day.

Then, all of the sudden, Hayley turns around and calls out to Violette, "You are so lucky!"

Violette sweetly smiles at both the girls and squeezes Mathieu's hand under the table. "I am lucky, indeed."

Once alone again, Violette stares at him in pure amazement and asks, "Does this happen often?"

"Yep!" He takes a giant bite of falafel and wipes the tzatziki sauce from his chin.

"I can't believe no one recognized you before." She takes a small, dainty bite out of her sandwich.

"I was sneaky!" he says. "That's why I was always wearing caps and sunglasses when I went outside with you."

"Oh. I thought you were a vampire."

Mathieu laughs. "Do the fans bother you?"

"No, I'm fascinated!"

"Well, it's still me, just Mathieu. Don't let the fame go to your head," he teases. "I really want to see all the work that you've done over at my house. I haven't been back since I left you there. What do you say, after we eat lunch, we venture over there?"

"Sounds good to me."

"Oh, and by the way, you are famous by association, so get used to the paparazzi, little lady!"

When they get to Mathieu's house, Mathieu admires all the work Violette did.

"I thought the pictures were awesome, but all of this? It's incredible! Violette, this is amazing, truly spectacular."

He walks from room to room, running his hands along the textures of the different fabrics, admiring the draperies, repeating how cool all of the accent pieces are and how beautiful the artwork is. The house feels cozy, but it still has a bit of Mathieu's edge. He grins at her, knowing that she got him. She even had all his guitars mounted on one wall, displaying them like art pieces.

When he is through with the house tour, he embraces Violette and kisses her. "You have a seriously awesome knack for this decorating thing."

"Thanks! I had fun doing it."

With seriousness and earnestness, he asks, "So is it still your dream home?"

"It's still my dream home," she says with definite certainty.

He asks her to stay with him, and she can't refuse. She wants to spend every second possible with this guy. First, she needs to run to her place and grab some essentials.

Violette quickly drives over her place, and when she arrives back at Mathieu's house, the place is dark. No lights are on.

"That's odd," Violette says, putting her car in park and turning the engine off. She walks to the front porch, puts the key in the lock, and turns it. She twists the doorknob to the right, and when she opens the door, she laughs and smiles, feeling curious about what her leading man is up to now.

She looks around the room and realizes that none of the furniture is there. Instead, a mountain of blankets and a sea pillows and white tea light candles are scattered throughout. It looks just as it did on their first date, the night that Mathieu bought the house and they celebrated with a dinner picnic on this very floor. The only difference is that he scattered rose petals from pink, red, and white flowers all over the room.

"Mathieu?" she calls out, taking a couple steps into the room now.

"Hang on!" He sounds as though he is in a distant room. "I'm coming!"

When he appears in the living room, he walks over to her, grabs her hand, and pulls her into the center of the room. For a moment, Violette wonders what in the world is going on. Then he pulls out a little square black box from his pocket. With great ease, he lowers his body and gets down on one knee. Violette cannot believe what is happening.

"Violette Deschamps, I know you are the girl for me. We haven't known each other that long. We haven't even gone on that many dates. This is crazy, I know. But, please, make me the happiest man in France, in all the world, and be my bride. Violette Deschamps, will you marry me?"

He opens the ring box and looks nervously and expectantly at Violette.

She stands there, her mouth gaping. She takes in this picture of her life, wanting to freeze-frame it for all eternity. She stares at Mathieu, a tear in her eye, and she can hardly speak. Of all the things that could have happened, this is a total surprise. There have been no talks of marriage and no hints or cues he was even thinking about it. He hadn't even said he loved her yet.

"Violette, say something, please." Mathieu is looking a little uneasy.

"Oh, yes! Sorry! Yes, I'll marry you. I love you, Mathieu Deneuve."

"I love you, Violette." He takes the ring out of the box, and she holds out her hand. "Forever and ever."

He slides the ring on her finger, and it actually fits. "The future Mrs. Mathieu Deneuve."

"I like how that sounds." She beams at him and looks down at her finger. "Mathieu, this ring is beautiful." She has been so focused on Mathieu and the moment that she has barely paid attention to the sparkling diamond on her finger until she looks down on it.

They never talked about rings, but it is truly perfect, a classic, like Violette herself. The ring is a simple circle diamond, generous in size, set in a white gold band.

"This feels unreal," Violette says. "Like something out of a movie."

"What would you know about movies?" Mathieu says.

"Oh I've been catching up. What do you think I do in my spare time now?"

"I have one more surprise for you."

"Another surprise? Are you just trying to send me into cardiac arrest?" She snuggles close into his chest.

Mathieu pulls a set of keys from his pocket and tells her that they have an errand to run, and it's a surprise.

"What if I guess where we are going?" she asks from the passenger seat of the car.

"Nope."

"Can we play twenty questions?"

"Nope," he says. "But wait, aren't you doing that now?"

"Ha, ha, very funny, mister."

Violette doesn't even know where they are, but finally, Mathieu pulls his car into the parking lot of a small brick building.

"Where the heck are we?" Violette asks. Before he answers, she sees a small sign on the side of the building: *Animal Rescue.*

She looks excitedly at Mathieu. "What does this mean? Does this mean what I think it means?"

"I thought we could get a present to celebrate our engagement," he says with a mischievous look.

She protests, "But my ring is my present." She waves her finger in the air.

"I want you to have everything in life that you could ever possibly want. You said you wanted a dog, so I thought we could pick out one from the shelter. I believe your exact words were you want a goldendoodle or a rescue pound puppy. So, today, any of these dogs that you want are going to be part of our new family."

Violette loves the way he emphasizes the word *our*, and she loves that she has a new family to be part of.

"Okay!" She happily obliges, feeling childlike.

They walk into the shelter and are greeted by a volunteer who takes them to the dog kennels, with rows of dogs of all shapes and sizes and colors in cages. They wag their tails, bark, and vie for attention. Violette is instantly drawn to a reddish-brown dog who calmly peers at them. She reads the tag by his cage, "Rover, age three, stray, redbone coonhound mix." The pup is maybe forty pounds, she guesses, and has white paws and a white tip on his tail. The volunteer leashes him, and they walk him around outside on a small path.

Rover is so excited and lovable and can't stop playing with Mathieu or Violette. Violette knows this sweet bundle of dog is the perfect fit for the new family that they are starting. Mathieu does too. "So is this the one?"

"He's the one!"

After filling out their paperwork, Rover gets a couple of shots and a "welcome home" basket from the shelter filled with toys and a starter bag of dog food. They bring him home, to their home, and Violette's heart feels as though it's expanding. Her happiness soars, and she cannot believe that she is finally getting her happy Hollywood movie ending.

That night, Rover, Mathieu, and Violette spend the first night of the rest of their lives together. Violette feels safe and secure, a feeling that had been lost since her mother's passing. They are a totally normal couple doing totally normal things. They make dinner, they play with the dog, they watch TV, and they steal kisses from one another.

During the commercials of one of the shows, Mathieu turns and tells Violette, "So, let's share the good news." He e-mails his sister, Madeleine, and next up, he calls his parents.

"Hey, Mom, it's Mathieu." He touches the speaker button on his phone when she answers so that Violette can hear the conversation too.

"Mathieu! Darling! How are you? Hang on, let me get your dad."

"Good to hear from you, boy," his dad says.

"We miss you!" His parents are talking so much, he can barely get a word in.

"Are you ready?" he mouths to Violette. She nods her head. "Well, I have some news."

"More tours?" his mom says. "We love your new single, by the way. Your dad can't stop humming it." He can hear the pride in his mother's voice.

"Actually, it's not about music. I am engaged, actually."

"No!" his mom says. "I don't believe you!"

"Believe it!" He chuckles. "She's here with me, say hello to future the Mrs. Mathieu Deneuve, Violette Deschamps."

"Hi," Violette shyly says.

"This is a shock, but welcome to the family, Violette," his dad says. "We can't wait to meet you!"

"Have you set a date? Are you going to do it here in Paris?" His mother sounds even more eager.

"No date yet, but I want to do it soon. Why wait? I would elope tonight if Violette would agree to it."

"Mathieu, don't you dare do that. Your mama needs to see you say I do!"

"No, no, I already know Violette wants a small, beautiful wedding. Whatever she wants, she'll have."

Mathieu and his parents talk a million miles an hour and work on planning a time to get together. Violette sits back and enjoys being part of a family again. Today she has added many new titles to her personal résumé: fiancée, future daughter-in-law, and future sister-in-law, and, as Rover curls up beside her, the title of dog mom.

As the newly engaged couple sits by the fire, chatting with Mathieu's family and sharing their good news, Violette realizes that dreams do come true and that change happens when you least expect it.

From nights alone with red wine and mystery books, to snuggling up with Mathieu and Rover, Violette sighs contently, leans into her man's chest, and soaks in every second of her fairy-tale ending.

CHAPTER TWENTY-SEVEN

Six weeks after the fateful day at the radio station, Mathieu and Violette have finished moving the last box into her new office... and they are exhausted.

"Rover, roll over!" Mathieu commands the furry dog, and he obliges.

Rover enthusiastically rolls over and looks up to his parents for a cookie. Rover has become the official mascot of Violette's new interior design business, Deschamps Domaines. He is featured on the company logo.

Violette carries in the last box and turns to her two favorite guys. "So, what do you think?"

"It's perfect," he says, looking around the brand-new Deschamps Domaines office space.

There are four showrooms highlighting the season's newest trends in kitchens, bathrooms, living rooms, and bedrooms, an office room with top-of-the-line CAD software, and a reception area where her new assistant will be working.

Violette cannot believe how quickly her business has grown, and she is loving every second of it. It's true what they say, if you love what you do, you never work a day in your life. Violette's new career epitomizes this.

This weekend, with the help of Marcel, Guillaume, and Olivier, they moved Violette into her new office space, and they also moved Violette out of her flat and into Chateau Deneuve, their nickname for their home, their slice of paradise.

She put her apartment up for sale, using Jean-Philippe as her realtor, and it was sold within a few weeks, record time for her Parisian suburb area. A girl very similar to Violette will be moving in—young, single, and full of dreams.

Violette is so thankful for the experiences that shaped her. Her own flat was magical to her. It whetted her appetite for design and was always there for her through the good and bad times.

She will miss her old place, but she looks forward to making memories with Mathieu and Rover in the years to come. She used to think her life would begin once she found love. She realizes now that her life had already begun, something she hopes the new homeowner will learn at an earlier age than Violette did. Life begins when you choose for it to begin.

"All right, Miss Violette, are you ready to go home?"

Home.

There is no place she would rather be than home with her Mathieu and her Rover. Mathieu and Les Slinks are leaving for a three-month tour around European, and Violette is staying back with Rover to keep her business going. Violette will join him for a few of the shows to see all the behind-the-scenes hoopla and watch him perform in a concert... her first one. They'll get to play tourists, and Mathieu can't wait to show her some of his favorite places in Ireland, Holland, and Greece. This is literally a whole new world for his bride-to-be.

Paris's new *it* couple is all the rage in the media, especially as they plan their wedding. Mathieu has told Violette that he knows the perfect place to hold a wedding: The Little Rose Bed and Breakfast. When Mathieu picked up his stuff from the inn, he felt so bad about the hard times the Beland family had fallen into. The buzz of the Deneuve wedding there will hopefully drum up some business for Elle and Albert. And when Violette saw the beautiful grounds, she said it would be perfect. It was exactly the type of setting she wanted for a small, quaint wedding. Although he doesn't always let it show, Mathieu knows that name-dropping and using his fame can sometimes help others. That alone is worth the price of fame.

Violette takes one more look around her new shop and can't wait to come back tomorrow. But tonight, she and Mathieu are spending one more quiet night at home. He is making his homemade marinara sauce for her, the one he keeps talking up. As she turns the lights off at the new shop, Violette smiles to herself. Home is where the heart is. As she leaves for the night, she whispers, "You're going home, Violette. You're going home."

ABOUT THE AUTHOR

Chloe Emile writes sweet, clean romance, whether it's contemporary or historical. She can usually be found working on her next novel, eating takeout with her husband, or watching rom-coms.

Visit her website for the latest updates.

www.ChloeEmile.com

Chloe Emile